JO ANN YHARD

LOST

on Brier Island

Happy Adventures!

NIMBUS
PUBLISHING LTD

Nimbus Publishing Limited
3731 Mackintosh St, Halifax, NS B3K 5A5
(902) 455-4286 nimbus.ca

Printed and bound in Canada
Design: Kate Westphal, Graphic Detail Inc.
Author photo: Rhonda Basden

Library and Archives Canada Cataloguing in Publication

Yhard, Jo Ann
Lost on Brier Island / Jo Ann Yhard.
ISBN 978-1-55109-819-7
I. Title.

PS8647.H37L68 2011   jC813'.6   C2011-900031-8

Nimbus Publishing acknowledges the financial support for its publishing activities from the Government of Canada through the Canada Book Fund (CBF) and the Canada Council for the Arts, and from the Province of Nova Scotia through the Department of Communities, Culture and Heritage.

To my family.

I am grateful for your continued support

and inspiration, especially to our next

generation—Mary, Matthew, and Ella.

You keep us all young at heart.

CHAPTER ONE

ALEX SAT IN THE KITCHEN with her arms crossed and stared at the red and white checked pattern on the tablecloth. Her stomach growled. Out of the corner of her eye, she could see Aunt Sophie approaching in her paint-splattered jeans.

"C'mon, kiddo, eat up." Aunt Sophie placed a plate of scrambled eggs in front of her. "These are eggs like you never tasted—from my own chickens."

"Not hungry."

Her aunt sighed and sat down.

Alex turned away and looked out the window at the ocean off in the distance.

"Alexandra," Aunt Sophie said, "I can live with the grumpy face, but you have to eat." She pushed the plate closer and plunked a glass of apple juice down beside it.

"Don't want it." Alex nudged her chair away from the table. "And my name is Alex."

"Alex, then. You've been here for two days already. You can't keep sneaking the cookies and pop I bought as a treat for you and not eat regular meals."

Alex's head snapped up in surprise.

"Hey, I can see when a cookie box is empty as well as anyone." Aunt Sophie smiled. "Sorry, kiddo, I've got to pull out the responsible adult act here. You'll just have to sit there until you finish it."

"Fine!" Alex scowled and stabbed her fork at the yellow mound, stuffing in a mouthful. The eggs were soft and creamy. Her stomach growled even louder.

"See, it's not so bad." Aunt Sophie patted her shoulder and got up from the table. "Besides, you need your strength. It's a sunny day, finally. We're going out."

Alex gulped down the cold juice. Out? She couldn't think where they would go. Brier Island had no mall, no movie theatre, and no arcade. There was nothing at all to do.

They strolled down the dirt road. Aunt Sophie didn't drive unless she had to. Alex could see a sketch pad peeking out from her aunt's bag. *Hmmm, she's probably going to try to get me drawing again*, Alex thought. Her aunt was wasting her time.

"Oh, look." Aunt Sophie stopped suddenly and pointed to a cluster of yellow flowers by the side of the road. "These are endangered."

Endangered flowers? That was silly. They looked like plain old buttercups—nothing special about that. A fat bumblebee droned past her and landed on one of the yellow petals.

"What a great shot," Aunt Sophie said. She pulled her camera from her bag and started snapping away. "So unusual, too—I've only seen Eastern Mountain Avens in Big Meadow in the nature preserve."

Alex glanced across the field at the water. She could hear waves crashing against the shore. The sun was warm.

She tilted her head back and closed her eyes. The rays felt good on her face.

After a few minutes, Alex noticed the camera had stopped whirring and clicking. She opened her eyes to see what her aunt was doing.

Aunt Sophie was staring at her with a weird expression on her face. Was she going to cry?

"What's wrong?" Alex glanced back over her shoulder. There was nothing but the flowers, the cliff, and the ocean.

"What?" Aunt Sophie seemed to snap out of a trance. "Oh, it's nothing. I thought…it looked like you were almost smiling there for a minute. It caught me by surprise."

Alex didn't say anything and resumed walking. Her aunt kept pace beside her. They travelled in silence for a while. Butterflies and bees continued to cross their path.

"You know, if you want to talk—"

"I don't," Alex said. She clenched her hands and started walking faster, almost tripping in her sneakers. They were dark blue and a size too big. Dust from the road billowed around her.

"Okay, slow down! Forget I said anything."

Alex ignored her, practically running now.

"Please stop, Alex." Her aunt jogged beside her. "I promise I won't mention it again." She touched Alex's arm. "I promise."

Alex slowed down and let out a deep breath. An old man riding a bicycle smiled and waved at them as he passed by. The bicycle was rusty with huge tires. It looked like it was from a museum. So did the man. With his frail hands and wispy white hair, he looked like he was made of parchment paper.

"Hi, Henry." Aunt Sophie waved back.

Alex didn't wave or smile.

The tide was out. Mustard-coloured seaweed covered the rocky shore like a blanket. A bright white and black seagull sat amongst the thick strands, its beak clamped around a purple mussel.

Not that long ago, Alex would have been reaching for the coloured pencils and sketch pad that she always used to keep with her.

Instead, her gaze was drawn to the ferry as it sped away from the dock towards Long Island. Only one thought was in her head.

How could she sneak on board and escape from this island prison?

CHAPTER TWO

"HI, EVA. WHAT FLAVOUR COFFEE have you got on today?" Aunt Sophie asked as they entered the café. She tossed her bag onto the counter and made a beeline for the coffee perk.

"Bavarian cinnamon. I thought it would go great with my gooseberry scones, fresh out of the oven."

"Mmmm. Butter one up for me, would you?" Aunt Sophie grabbed a chipped green mug from the tray by the coffee and poured a steaming cup. The smell of cinnamon filled the room.

As Eva and her aunt chatted, Alex turned away to roam through the aisles of the general store section of the café. It was strange coming from Halifax, a city, where there were separate stores for clothes, food, and pharmacy stuff. Everything here was jammed together on neatly stacked shelves. Tomato soup sat next to rubber boots, diapers, and playing cards.

"Has Gus been in?" Sophie asked.

"Not yet," Eva said. "But I expect him any time. Thinking of going out today?"

"If he's not booked up with paying customers," Sophie said. "The fog and rain have cleared off, so it's a good chance to get some photographs of the humpbacks in the bay. I hear there have been some new arrivals."

"Yes, that's July for you," Eva said. "Here you go. I topped it off with my field berry jam."

"Wow, Eva, this is amazing!"

"Hi there, dear. Would you like a scone too?"

Alex was examining a tiny sewing kit, filled with mini spools of all different colours of threads.

"Alex?" Aunt Sophie said. "Eva is talking to you."

Reluctantly, Alex put the kit back on the shelf and walked over to the counter. "Sorry," she mumbled. She stared at the scones. Steam was still rising from the fluffy biscuits filled with bright berries.

"Try one," Eva said. "You'll think you died and went to heaven."

Alex gasped and backed away from the counter. She whirled around to flee and smacked into the movie rental rack. DVD and VHS cases tumbled to the floor as she tripped, falling to her knees.

"Dear lord, I didn't mean—"

"It's okay, Eva." Aunt Sophie knelt down beside Alex and grabbed her arms. "Are you all right?"

Alex shook her head and pushed her aunt's hands away. Tears blurred her vision.

The jingle of the hummingbird wind chimes over the screen door made her jump. Huge scuffed work boots stopped in front of her. Alex blinked and looked up. Golden hazel eyes stared back at her, surrounded by a mane of bushy brown hair speckled with grey.

"Morning, Sophie. I take it this is your summer visitor?" The man's voice was deep and gravelly, like the low growl of a lion.

"Hi, Gus." Aunt Sophie stood up, tugging Alex with her. "This is Alex. Alex, this is Gus."

"Pleased to meetcha." A hand the size of a plate stretched out towards her.

Alex was mesmerized by the thick digits and unexpected perfectly trimmed, white fingernails. Lions had claws, didn't they? She didn't move.

"Bogs!" Gus grabbed her hand and pumped it up and down.

Alex's teeth chattered as her whole body vibrated.

"So, want to see some whales, eh?"

"Whales?" Alex turned to her aunt. "What's he talking about?"

"Don't be rude," Aunt Sophie said. "Yes, Gus, we do, if you've got room."

"Yup, only two booked in 'cause of the weather lately—plenty of space." He turned away and plunked a large travel mug on the counter. "Eva, fill 'er up with some tea, would ya? Normal leaded tea, now. None of that herb crap." He bent down over the scones and sniffed. "And toss a couple of these biscuits in too."

"Crap indeed!" Eva muttered as she went about getting Gus's order packed up.

Alex trudged along behind Gus and Aunt Sophie as the three of them crossed the road and walked the short distance to the dock. She carried a paper bag filled with scones that Eva had insisted she take. "You'll get hungry out there," she had said.

They passed fishing huts that extended out over the shoreline. The tiny buildings looked like old wooden garages on stilts, towering above the rocks. Their criss-crossed support beams were covered almost entirely with seaweed and barnacles. Alex was shocked. The tide didn't go that high, did it?

She trod carefully on the wharf where Gus's boat was moored. The wooden planks were uneven and many didn't seem to be nailed down. She almost fell twice when her loose sneakers caught on a beam that popped up when she stepped on it.

Her heart beat faster and her footsteps slowed as she approached the boat, bobbing on the water. It was shiny and looked new. An older couple was standing there waiting. Alex's attention was drawn back to the boat. She had never been on one that small before. The ferry had been bad enough, and it was much bigger.

Her brother Adam's teasing voice echoed in her head. *Hey, wuss, you don't swim so great, remember? Don't fall in!*

She stumbled on the first step and froze, staring down at the dark water as it lapped between the vessel and the dock. Her breath caught in her throat.

It seemed like a big gap to her—too big.

CHAPTER THREE

"TIME'S A-WASTIN'," GUS SAID. "What's the problem?"

"Nothing." Alex couldn't stop staring down at the space between the boat and the dock. She felt dizzy. Was it getting wider? What if she slipped and fell in?

"Bogs!" Gus said. His two plate-sized hands reached over, scooped her up, and plopped her down on the deck.

"Don't touch me!" Alex backed away from him. The deck moved beneath her feet and she wobbled slightly.

"Haven't got all day." Gus gazed down at her for another second before turning and walking through the glassed-in cabin to an open door leading to the wheelhouse. Another, shorter, man was already at the controls.

Aunt Sophie was babbling away with the older couple, oblivious to Alex's plight. Some guardian she was. Lion man could have tossed her overboard. Alex spied the bright red life jackets and put one on. Her heartbeat slowly returned to normal. At least she wouldn't drown.

She retreated to the back of the boat and sat on the cushioned bench that lined the sides of the open deck. She pulled her bent legs into her chest and wrapped her arms around them. Leaning forward, she rested her chin on her knees and stared at the shimmering water.

soon they were chugging out of the harbour. Gus pointed to great blue herons perched in the trees along the shoreline. Alex had never seen one in real life, just on television. They looked like exotic birds from the Amazon rainforest.

The waves got choppier as they rounded the lighthouse and headed into open water. It was colder, too. The life jacket didn't do anything to stop the wind. Alex shivered and hugged her knees more tightly to her chest.

"Give Alex one of my sweaters, would ya, Soph? There's a stack over on the bench," Gus bellowed from the wheelhouse. "Grab one for yourself too."

Did he have ESP? Alex wondered. Or maybe eyes in the back of his head? How did he know she was cold? She didn't turn around as a knitted sweater was wrapped around her shoulders.

"Put it on, it'll keep you nice and toasty," Aunt Sophie said. "Sorry, I forgot to bring jackets."

The sweater was scratchy against her arms, which made sense since it belonged to Gus, the lion man. Scratchy, like she imagined lion fur would be. She didn't put it on but didn't shrug it off, either. At least it was warm.

Gus joined them on the open deck. "Got my nephew at the controls today. Susan, our biologist, is out sick, so you're stuck with me."

The couple was asking Gus an endless stream of questions. What kind of whales would they see? What other wildlife? How long had he been doing this? What did he do when tourist season was over?

Half listening, Alex learned that with luck they would see humpback, minke, and maybe fin whales. Sometimes, there were sightings of right whales, an endangered species. She also learned that Gus fished lobster in the off-tourist season.

"Why are they called right whales?" the woman asked.

Alex was wondering the same thing. It was kind of a weird name for a whale.

"It's sad, really," Gus said. "Whalers way back in the day named them that because they were the 'right' whale to hunt. They swam slowly and close to the surface, so they were easy to harpoon. And, because they had a thick blubber layer, it made them float after they were killed."

"Oh my goodness, how horrible!" the woman exclaimed.

Alex thought it was horrible too. Why did the whales do that? They should have been smart and swum faster and dove deeper. Then they wouldn't have gotten killed.

"Are you excited to see whales?" the woman asked her.

Alex didn't want to talk, but also didn't want to be embarrassed again by having Aunt Sophie call her rude. "Not really."

"Oh." The woman's smile faltered slightly. "Why are you out here, then?"

"My aunt made me come," she said politely. Aunt Sophie frowned at her from across the deck, but didn't say anything. Well, what could she say? It was the truth, and she hadn't been rude.

...e." The woman's smile disappeared and she walked back over to stand beside Gus, resuming her questions.

Happy to be left alone, Alex looked towards the water again and gasped—she couldn't see a thing. Fog had crept in from nowhere and cocooned them in a world of white.

She heard Gus sigh at the same time the motor stopped. The boat drifted in silence. "Welcome to the Bay of Fundy!" he chuckled. "I had been hoping we would keep the sun, but apparently Mother Nature has other plans for us today."

"Do we get a refund?" the woman's husband asked. "We were guaranteed to see whales. Who can see anything in this pea soup?"

Gus didn't get angry. Alex figured this must have happened before. "Don't give up. We don't use any fancy equipment or anything to find the whales. It's just keen eyesight looking for blowholes on the horizon. When it's sunny, that is. In the fog, we'll have to use our ears. You can hear them when they blow."

The man frowned. "You've got to be kidding, right? Listen for whales on a whale watch?"

Gus smiled again, but Alex noticed his lips were more pressed together. She wondered what lion man was like when he got mad.

"We'll go ahead slowly for a bit, then stop, and we'll see what happens," he said, pausing to yell the instructions to his nephew. "Be patient. The whales have a big bay to swim around in and we didn't tie 'em up the last time we saw them. You never know where they'll turn up.

Besides, Bay of Fundy fog is a fickle lady—she could scurry off as quick as she came."

They cruised around for the next half hour, stopping every few minutes to listen for whale blows. Alex didn't even know what the sound was supposed to be. Not that she could have heard anything anyway. The man was complaining more loudly by the minute about what a waste of money the trip was, and that they should have gone golfing in Digby instead.

When the boat stopped again, Gus disappeared up to the viewing deck. Sophie and the woman were on the other side of the boat. No one was talking to the man, and he had gone into the sheltered cabin section of the boat and was reading a magazine.

This stinks, Alex thought. Plus, she was freezing. Looking around to make sure no one saw her, she pulled Gus's lion-fur sweater over her head. It fell below her knees and the arms drooped well past her hands. She rolled up the sleeves as best she could. Despite its scratchiness, the sweater was warm.

Wondering if she might be able to at least catch a glimpse of a nearby jellyfish through the fog, Alex leaned cautiously over the railing and peered down into the calm water.

A humungous eye was staring back at her.

Alex screamed.

CHAPTER FOUR

GUS LEAPT FROM ABOVE LIKE some kind of superhero and landed on the deck with a thud. "What happened?"

"Over there." Alex pointed a shaking finger. "There's something in the water!"

"Is that right?" Gus grinned and walked over to take a look.

"Watch out!" Alex couldn't help but cry. The thing was huge. What if it tipped their boat over? Or jumped up and knocked them into the water? She checked the ties on her life jacket to make sure they were still tight.

Gus started to laugh. "Well, well, we're in luck."

Alex thought he must really be crazy. He should be trying to get them away from this thing.

"Thanks to Alex, we have our first whale sighting." Gus beckoned everyone with a wave. "Come on over and say hi to Sockeye. He's a humpback, and he's one of our long-time visitors here in the bay."

The woman whizzed by Alex and leaned over the side of the boat. "Oh my," she gushed. She looked up at Gus and batted her eyes. "Are we in danger? It looks like he's under our boat!"

"We'll sue if anything happens!" her husband whined, striding over to stand beside her. He pointed at the water.

"That doesn't look like much. How can you even tell it's a whale? Aren't they supposed to jump around or something?"

Gus finally lost the hold he had seemed to have on his temper. "Good grief, man, will you button that flapping trap of yours!" he roared.

The man twitched and ducked behind his wife. Alex watched him fiddle with his camera. He reminded her of a yippy chihuahua that had been barked at by a bigger dog and then turned tail and run.

When it became clear the whale was no danger to the boat, Alex's panic receded. She felt the apathy seep back into her limbs like a drug. It was as if the cold fog had crept inside her and was spreading through her body, numbing her.

Sockeye apparently didn't feel like putting on a show, either. Maybe he felt as lonely as she did out here. He kept coming to the surface briefly and then vanishing into the depths again.

The fog had finally vanished from around the boat, too. It was there, and then it wasn't—like it was alive, toying with them. But it hadn't gone far. Alex could see it just off in the distance, waiting. It looked solid as a wall. Could it be a portal to another world? She wished.

They decided to move on and see who else was around. As the boat zigzagged around the bay, they came across a basking shark and a sunfish. There were tons of birds, too. Gus was rattling off their names—northern gannets, different kinds of shearwaters, and northern fulmars.

enly, the boat jerked forward and they were
..eaming across the choppy surface. "Blow holes at ten
o'clock!" Gus shouted, pointing to his left.

The couple whipped their matching binoculars up to
their eyes in perfect unison as Aunt Sophie grabbed her
camera.

What was all the fuss over more whales? Alex
wondered. It seemed like they'd been out on this floating
freezer for hours. Cold ocean spray from the speeding
boat matted her hair and coated her skin.

"There they are!" Aunt Sophie cried.

"Try and get pictures of the flukes, would ya, Soph?"
Gus asked. "We'll get them posted on the tracking
website."

"Tracking what?" asked the woman.

"Each tail is unique," Aunt Sophie explained, grabbing
a reference book. She opened it and pointed to one of the
pictures. "See here? The different patterns, shapes, and
markings on the tails are like fingerprints for whales. So,
by photographing the tails, the flukes, we can identify
the whales and track their migrations."

"That's extraordinary," the woman said.

"I know," Aunt Sophie replied. "Researchers all up and
down the East Coast post photos to log sightings. It's a very
effective way to track the whales. For instance, we know
Sockeye has been coming to the Bay of Fundy since 1984."

"But we didn't see his tail back there, or much of anything, for that matter," the man said. "How do you know
the name of it? Or even if it was a whale at all?"

Gus let out another menacing growl and the man twitched again. It was much more entertaining watching this show than the whales.

"Sockeye might not be the best example. He got his name because of his unique underbite, not his tail. It makes him look a bit like a sockeye salmon. One of a kind, that fella. We know him very well," Gus said. "Now, get ready. I think that's Rooftop and her calf."

An enormous black form exploded from the surface. It seemed to hover for just a second before crashing back into the water, followed almost immediately by a smaller whale mimicking the same move—a baby whale. Despite her bored expression, Alex could feel her pulse quicken.

The baby jumped and flipped and slapped and rolled, smacking its flippers on the surface, all actions Gus had mentioned they might see if they were lucky. He had also talked about spyhopping, when whales poked their heads out of the water to take a look around. But spyhopping was a much quieter activity, and the baby whale seemed too excited for quiet, continuing to explode high into the air.

Alex leaned against the railing and watched the show. Rooftop, the mother, eventually seemed to get tired of all her baby's antics. She moved farther away from the boat, resting quietly on the surface.

"What's the baby's name?" the woman asked.

"He doesn't have one yet," Gus explained. "The humpback calves are about seven months old and won't get an official name until they return to the bay on their own."

"Rooftop's calf is a real daredevil, though," Gus added. "I've never seen anything like it—disappearin' from its mother's side all the time. That's dangerous behaviour for such a young whale."

Daredevil. That's what Mom had always called Adam, too. Mom would laugh when she said it, though. So would Adam. Then Mom would ruffle his hair while he tried to squirm away. Her brother had always gotten into trouble, and that had usually meant trouble for Alex, too. He'd get her dragged into his mess every time. She felt a lump form in her throat and sucked in a deep breath.

The ocean was so calm now that she wasn't nervous of the water anymore. Stretching her arms out, she could almost touch the surface. Thinking of Adam, Alex let out a heavy sigh and closed her eyes, her heart aching for things that couldn't be.

Alex jumped as something wet and smooth brushed against her outstretched hands. She gasped as she opened her eyes. The baby humpback's head was raised out of the water and it was totally still, watching her.

Holding her breath, Alex slowly ran her hands over its wet skin. The whale didn't move. This was the spyhopping Gus had talked about. Was the baby whale checking her out? Sounds faded away as the baby pushed its head gently up against her hands. The moment seemed to last forever.

The railing dug into her ribs, but she ignored it, leaning even farther. She kept stroking the baby's head— its skin was dark grey and it had a white shape like a sideways question mark over its right eye. Eventually, it sank back silently beneath the surface.

Alex stayed perfectly still, staring intently at the water until all the ripples had disappeared.

"Bye, Daredevil," she whispered.

CHAPTER FIVE

ALEX LET OUT THE BREATH she had been holding and stood up. She stretched her back, then reached under the scratchy sweater and life jacket to massage her tender ribs. Her eyes happened to drift upward and she was startled to see Gus smiling down at her from the observation deck. He gave her a brief salute before disappearing from view. Had he seen her with Daredevil?

She would rather no one had—then it would be her secret. Everyone seemed to know every teeny tiny scrap about her life these days. Alex sat down and opened the bag of scones Eva had given her. They were already buttered and slathered with homemade jam. Starving, Alex gulped one down, then another. Her eyes scanned the water's surface, but there was no sign of either Rooftop or Daredevil.

Licking the last traces of tart jam from her fingers, Alex realized she was thirsty, too. Maybe Aunt Sophie had packed something. Sitting cross-legged on the bench, she rested the bag in her lap and flipped it open. Inside was a book on wildflowers and other plants of Brier Island, a book on whale watching, and a hand-drawn map of the island covered in her aunt's funky handwriting.

Tucked in the bottom were a small sketchbook and an eight-pack of her favourite drawing pencils. There was a note attached.

Alex — in case you get the itch to explore...
and maybe sketch something! ☺

Alex crumpled the note and threw everything back into the bag. So what if she didn't want to draw?

She stuffed the bag under the bench and stared off at the looming fog bank as they steamed back to the island. It seemed to follow them. The boat slowed again and pulled up to idle beside a place called Seal Cove. It wasn't hard to tell why. There were seals everywhere. Big brown ones lounged on the long, flat rocks closer to shore, with smaller, lighter-coloured ones close by— baby seals. A few lifted their heads to check out the boat and its occupants.

More seals popped up around the boat. Alex looked into the warm liquid eyes of one that had surfaced beside her. She wondered what it would say to her if it could speak. They stayed there for a while, drifting as they listened to the seals barking at each other. That's what Gus called it, and it did sound like barking. Then the fog enveloped them again. Time was up, and Gus's nephew steered them back towards port.

The harbour was still and silent as they eased into the mooring. Alex breathed a sigh of relief. The boat had started to feel claustrophobic. She needed to get off, to get away from the closeness. Gus had barely tied on the lines when she leapt onto the wharf. It felt good to stand on something that wasn't moving.

"Hi, Uncle Gus."

Alex jumped. A tiny girl was standing behind her. She hadn't even noticed her.

"Hi, Rachel," Gus called out. He waved at her. "You missed the boat tour."

"I know. We were too late for the early ferry this morning. It was all Mom's fault."

Gus let out a belly laugh that rumbled through the air like thunder. A startled seagull took flight from the pole next to the boat. "Does your mum know that? I'm sure it had nothing to do with you!"

Rachel stuck her tongue out at him and then jumped onto the boat into his outstretched arms. Gus engulfed her in a tight bear hug. "It's good to see you again, squirt! You've grown since I was out there in February."

"Yup, I'm definitely taller!" Rachel said. "I'm going to be thirteen soon, too." She hopped down and prowled around the deck. "Ooh, I love the new boat, Uncle Gus. What did you name her?"

"Yup, she's a beauty," he agreed. "Welcome aboard the *Evania Rose*. Still have to paint the name on her, though."

"Can I go out with you tomorrow?"

"I think we can squeeze you in," Uncle Gus chuckled, ruffling Rachel's blonde curls. "If you behave, that is."

"Bogs!" Rachel growled.

What kind of a word was "bogs," anyway? Rachel sounded just like Gus. Great, Alex thought. Big lion and now little lion.

"Who are you?" Rachel asked.

"What?" Startled, Alex realized Rachel's attention was now focused on her.

"I don't know you." Rachel scrambled down to the dock and walked over to Alex.

Alex stepped back, but the girl kept coming closer. What was she going to do, walk right into her? Alex kept backing up until she was at the edge of the dock. Another step and she'd be in the harbour.

Obviously, this girl didn't know what personal space meant. There was nowhere left for Alex to go.

"Rachel, meet Sophie's niece, Alex," Gus said.

"Oh!" Rachel stared at her with big eyes. "You're that girl whose brother died."

CHAPTER SIX

WHAT DID SHE SAY? ALEX'S body went rigid.

"RACHEL!" Gus exclaimed.

"What? That's right, isn't it? Mom told me about her." Rachel tilted her head towards Alex. "You are her, aren't you?"

Alex pushed past her. She didn't wait for Aunt Sophie as she tripped down the wharf, her sneakers slipping as she went.

"Hey, what's the matter?" Rachel's voice followed her.

This was a mistake, Alex thought. She had told her parents she didn't want to come here, but they said it would be good for her. Yeah, right! They just wanted to get rid of her. Alex stomped along the road in the direction of the ferry, which had just docked. Four cars and a motorcycle drove off slowly and turned right, up the hill towards the lodge.

One red pickup was waiting to board. A bald man with a grey moustache was leaning out the window, talking to one of the ferry workers. He was lucky to be getting off this rock. Alex dug around in her pockets and pulled out three quarters, a nickel, and a gum wrapper. Not enough. What would she do when she got to the other side, anyway? Hitchhike? Maybe pickup-truck guy would give her a ride.

Hitching? Brave move, wuss. Bet you chicken out. Adam's voice echoed in her head. She gulped and stepped closer to the two men talking. "Um, excuse me?"

They both looked at her. "Afternoon," the ferry worker said. He squinted at her. "Don't I know you? Yeah, you're Sophie's niece, aren't ya?"

"Sophie's niece, eh? Welcome." The truck guy smiled.

"She came over the other day."

"How do you like our little island?"

Realizing that she'd been recognized and her chance of hitching a ride was now zero, Alex grudgingly answered the truck guy. "All right, I guess."

"Hmmm, that's not very enthusiastic," he chuckled. "I guess we can't compete with malls and movie theatres from the big city. Don't blame you, I s'pose. We old folks kind of like the peace and quiet."

"It's okay." Alex shrugged. She eventually made her escape after several more questions and hand waves.

Was there anyone Aunt Sophie didn't know? It was a bizarre feeling, like spies were watching her every move. In Halifax, no one knew who anyone was or cared what they did. Here, everyone knew each other and talked to each other, and waved to each other—all the time. Too weird.

Alex was anxious to get off the street and out of sight in case Rachel tried to follow her. She veered onto an old dock, towards one of the garages on stilts she'd passed by earlier. It looked abandoned. She carefully stepped over broken boards and walked behind the tiny building. A faded and peeling sign, *Robichaud Fishing*, leaned against the back wall. Alex sat down beside it and draped her legs over the edge of the wharf. Her loose sneakers dangled from the tips of her toes as she rocked her legs back and forth and gazed out to sea.

The tide was coming in. Fog was again crawling across the harbour, erasing land and water. The silence thickened and settled on her skin along with the cool foggy mist. She was finally alone. Alex let out a deep breath and felt her body start to relax.

It didn't last.

The girl whose brother died. Images of Adam flickered in her head: laughing, riding his bike with no hands down the hill, teasing her, pulling her up the tree behind him, skateboarding, and then lying pale and still in that hospital bed.

Alex shuddered. She could feel it rising again. Rising up from her gut like the high tide. Guilt.

It was relentless—eroding her like the waves crashing against the rocks, only from the inside out. It had all been her fault. If only she had been more like him, less of a chicken. She was transported away from the dock and back in time, lost inside her memories.

"Alex? Where are you?" Aunt Sophie's panicked yell echoed through the fog.

"Don't worry, she can't have gone far," Gus said. "I'll check Robichaud's here, Soph. Why don't you check the next one?"

Alex heard the creak of boards behind her. She didn't turn around as she felt Gus sit down beside her, his long legs stretching out over the edge of the wharf.

He pushed a large folded white cloth into her hand.

Alex held it away from her and looked up.

"Don't worry, it's clean," Gus laughed, seeming to read her mind.

Alex wiped the tears from her cheeks and eyes. Sniffing, she handed it back to Gus and continued to stare out at the wall of white.

"Fascinating, isn't it? The fog here is like a living thing," Gus said.

Alex nodded.

"Many a sailor have lost their way in fog like this. I've been tricked by the old girl myself on occasion—always found my way back, though, eventually." Gus's deep gravelly voice was soothing.

They sat in silence for a bit longer.

"We can't stay here, Alex. Your aunt is worried about you." Gus stood up and held out his hand.

Reluctantly, she reached up and let him tug her to her feet. "Thanks," she muttered.

He smiled and patted her shoulder. "Why don't you come out again tomorrow? Rachel speaks her mind, but she's a good kid. Besides, you might see your little whale buddy again."

So he had seen her after all. Well, she guessed she wouldn't mind seeing Daredevil again. And maybe she could ignore Rachel—she ignored lots of other things.

CHAPTER SEVEN

"ALEXANDRA—I MEAN, ALEX—YOU can't run off like that!"

Alex sat on the couch while Aunt Sophie paced back and forth.

"It's not that I don't trust you, but you know your mother. If anything happened to you…"

"I had to get away from her."

"Who? Rachel?"

"I don't like her."

Aunt Sophie sat on the edge of the couch. "She's a nice girl. And she's close to your age. I was hoping you two would hit it off."

"Oh yeah, best friends."

"You can't spend all your time alone, Alex. It's not good for you."

Alex scowled.

"Bottling up your emotions isn't good either," Aunt Sophie continued. "It's eating you up."

"You don't know how I feel."

"Alex, I was there…before Adam died. When you weren't at the hospital, you were locked away in his bedroom. You didn't talk to anyone for days at a time. Colleen told me that you were even worse after the funeral.

That's why your parents wanted you to come here—to get away from that. They were worried."

"Sure they were!" Alex could feel her head starting to throb.

"I'm not your enemy, Alex. I'm trying to help you."

"It doesn't seem like it. You sound just like my parents." Alex sprang to her feet and began pacing as her aunt had done. "They think it was my fault!"

Aunt Sophie's mouth dropped open. "That's not true!"

"It *is* true. You weren't there. You didn't see the way they looked at me." Alex could hear her voice shaking. "That's why they got rid of me."

"Got rid of you? You're wrong. There are other things going on, things you don't understand. Your mom and dad—"

"Stop it!" Alex choked. She couldn't take it anymore. "You promised you wouldn't talk about it."

"Okay, I'm sorry. You're right, I did promise."

"I'm going to my room." How normal she sounded. It didn't match at all the voice screaming inside her head.

"Wait, I'll make some dinner."

"No thanks."

"Alex…"

"Just leave me alone!" Alex ran up the stairs and slammed her door. She flopped on the bed and jammed on her headphones. Music blared from her MP3 player as she lay back on one of the pillows. She clutched the other pillow in her arms and held it tightly to her chest. Her heart jackhammered against her ribs.

Alex felt like a hamster that had been running on a wheel for months without stopping. She was so tired. Her body ached all over—even her eye sockets felt bruised. The music was calming. She listened to her whole playlist, two hours' worth, lying perfectly still.

By the end of the last tune, she had memorized every detail of the ceiling, including the brown water stain in the far corner, the sliver of mismatched blue paint around the edge of the light fixture, and the thin gossamer strand of a spider web clinging to an old brass hook screwed into the plaster. It swayed gently on the faint breeze drifting in from the open window.

Reaching under the pillow behind her head, Alex pulled out the photograph she kept tucked away. It was a picture of her and Adam at their eleventh birthday party three years ago. Alex let her mind drift back. The cake had been the best one ever. Her mom had decorated half of it green and blue with a skateboarder and the other half purple with a figure skater.

A figure skater, which didn't mean Alex was one. Not like Adam, who loved to skateboard. Not that he was allowed to have one back then. But he'd always wanted one, finally getting his wish at thirteen. Alex liked to watch figure skating on television and go see the skating shows at the Metro Centre. That was her—the watcher.

She ran her fingertip gently over Adam's laughing face. "I miss you," she whispered.

Alex rolled over on her side and closed her eyes. Her last thought was of Daredevil as she drifted off to sleep.

CHAPTER EIGHT

"GOOD MORNING, SWEETIE." EVA'S EYES twinkled at her from behind the counter. "Want some breakfast? I made something special this morning."

Sweetie? Alex blushed under Eva's direct gaze. "I *am* kind of hungry," she murmured.

"Of course, you're a growing girl!" Eva bustled. "I've got these ham and cheese rolls, my own concoction. Like a cinnamon roll—only better." She winked and handed one over the counter.

"Thanks, um, Ms…"

"Call me Eva, dear, everyone does. Tell me if you like it, and be honest." Eva wagged her finger. "I need to know if it's good enough."

"Good enough for what?"

"Eva's writing a cookbook of her own recipes," Aunt Sophie said. She set her already half-empty coffee cup on the counter and took a roll from Eva's outstretched hand.

"You're making your own cookbook?" Alex asked.

It was Eva's turn to blush. "Well now, I don't know. Sophie's been after me—said she'd do photos of the food for a book if I write up my recipes. I'm just putting a few together, that's all. We'll see what happens."

Alex took a bite, and immediately another. The buttery pastry melted in her mouth, blended with bits of salty ham and sharp cheddar.

Eva's cheeks bloomed even brighter. "I'll take that as a positive endorsement."

Alex stuffed the rest into her mouth. She suddenly remembered she hadn't eaten supper last night. "Can I have another one?"

"Well, how can I refuse? Not now that you're my official taste-tester."

"She's right, too!" Aunt Sophie said. "These definitely have to go in the book."

"Mornin', ladies," Gus called from the doorway. His huge frame blocked out the sunlight. "What's cookin'?"

He sat down at the only table in the small café section of the store. It was tall, with six high stools around it, and it sat in front of the large window. Gus pushed his wooden stool back to make room for his long legs. There was much chatter and laughter among Gus, Sophie, and Eva as they all feasted on coffee and rolls while Gus entertained them with one hilarious fishing story after another.

"Gus, stop!" Aunt Sophie gasped, holding her sides. Tears were running down her face. "I can't take it."

Gus grinned, but didn't let up. "And there was that little runt last season—no more than eighteen, I'd say. Remember him, Eva? Arty Leblanc's young fella, from over Long Island. Well, you shoulda seen him trying to get them lobsters out of the trap and get the claw bands on! There was a lobster clamped on his sleeve and another on his pant leg and he was runnin' around in a circle screaming like a baby. You'd a sworn he was getting eaten alive by dogfish or worse. Didn't last the day, that one!"

Alex could see the guy plain as day in her mind and she laughed. Surprised at the sound of her own laughter, she choked on her chocolate milk.

Gus slapped her back as she coughed. "Don't hurt yourself, now," he chuckled.

"All right there, dear?" Eva asked.

Sophie was watching her. Alex could feel the heat of embarrassment and then guilt creeping into her cheeks. Why had she laughed? She scowled and dropped her gaze, hunching down on her stool.

"Shouldn't you all be heading out now?" Eva finally said. She began gathering up the empty cups and plates.

"Right you are, Eva." Gus grabbed another roll. "Let's get a move on."

Alex slid off the stool and grabbed her pack. She'd made sure to bring a jacket this time. Aunt Sophie popped the last morsel into her mouth and took another drink of coffee.

"Aren't you coming?" Alex asked.

"Not today. I'm doing a painting demonstration in the gift shop."

"But...so I'm going alone?" Alex stood in the middle of the café, staring after Gus's lumbering form as he strode across the parking lot towards the wharf.

"Don't worry, Gus will take good care of you. Oh, I've got a favour to ask. Could you take my spare camera and get some fluke shots if you see any humpbacks today?"

"Me?"

"It's the Nikon," Sophie said, handing it over. "I showed you how to use it before. Remember?"

"Uh…"

"No sweat, I'll show you again." Aunt Sophie proceeded to give Alex a crash course that made her head spin. "See, it's easy!"

Alex repeated the instructions over and over in her head as she scurried down the wharf. There were two families and a couple already on board, and Rachel was inside with Gus.

They must be waiting for me, Alex thought. She barely looked down as she hopped over the gap between the dock and the boat and landed softly on deck.

"She's finally here, Uncle Gus." Rachel rolled her eyes.

Brat, Alex thought as the engine roared to life.

The bench that ran along the deck was full, so she stepped into the cabin area to the wheelhouse. She couldn't stand the thought of being surrounded by people.

"Gus, can I go up top?"

"Sure. Take your time and get up there now before we start moving. I've got the sound system on so you'll be able to hear me up there. No other help today. My marine biology student is still sick."

Alex slung her pack over her shoulder and climbed carefully up the metal ladder. Her loose sneakers slipped on the rungs, but she made it to the top. Securing a life jacket around her, she settled into one of the seats, more at ease than the day before. The boat slowly steamed out of the harbour and Alex watched for the herons she knew would be in the trees.

CHAPTER NINE

THE WIND WAS CHILLY. IT nipped her ears and made her eyes water. Alex took off the life jacket, shrugged into her windbreaker, and pulled the hood over her head, tightening the strings under her chin. She tugged on the bright vest again, tying it securely. Sunlight danced off the waves. The ocean had changed colour under a blue sky—now it was a rich cerulean rather than the slate grey of the foggy day before.

Alex hung Aunt Sophie's digital camera around her neck and snapped a few practice shots. She shaded the camera with her hand and hit the review button, disappointed to see the images were blurry and not quite centred. After several more attempts, the results were much better. Satisfied that she'd be ready when they came across whales, Alex turned her attention to the scenery.

There were tons of seabirds around. She pulled out the whale-watching book her aunt had given her and flipped to the small section on birds. She recognized a few from the previous day, then tried to identify some of the species flying about. She was able to match a greater shearwater and a northern fulmar to photos in the book.

The puffin was the cutest picture in the book, though. With its bright orange, rounded beak and puffed-out cheeks, it looked like a chubby parrot. Alex focused the binoculars on the bobbing seabirds, on the lookout for spots of bright orange.

"Alex, keep your eyes open for whale blows. You've got the best view. I'm sending Rachel up too," Gus's voice suddenly bellowed in her ear.

Alex jumped at the sudden, loud intrusion. She turned her head and noticed a speaker beside her, then caught Rachel's neon-yellow jacket out of the corner of her eye. She'd already climbed the ladder and was walking towards her.

"See anything yet?" Rachel asked.

Alex shrugged. "A few seabirds."

"Well, I'm a really good spotter, Uncle Gus said so. Just watch me!" Rachel chirped as she plopped down beside her.

"Uh-huh."

"Can I see your book?"

Alex passed it over.

Rachel flipped through the pages. "You should check out Uncle Gus's books. They have all kinds of birds. See, this book only has the greater shearwater. Did you know there's more than one kind of shearwater?"

"Uh-huh." *Who cares?* Alex thought. Her interest in the birds had evaporated with Rachel's arrival.

Rachel yammered on about all the different birds she'd seen that weren't in the book, whales she'd seen, when she'd seen them, and on and on. She didn't even seem to pause to take a breath. Alex was getting tired just listening to her.

"Are you ever quiet?"

"What do you mean?"

"You don't shut up!"

"That's a mean thing to say." Rachel frowned.

"Sorry. You talk too much. Is that better?" Alex said. "I was doing great up here alone."

"Well, excuse me for trying to be friendly!" Rachel huffed and tossed the book back at Alex.

Both of them looked off in different directions and didn't speak. Rachel didn't stop making noise, though. She sighed every ten seconds, getting louder each time. Alex tried to ignore her, but it was impossible.

Finally, it seemed Rachel couldn't hack not talking any longer. "I even brought you some lunch. I thought you'd be hungry."

"Why?"

Rachel bit her lip and avoided Alex's eyes. "Um, well I figured...you know, you're poor or something."

"What?" Alex gaped at her.

"Well, yesterday you didn't have a jacket—and those shoes." Rachel pointed to Alex's blue sneakers.

Alex lifted up her foot. "What's wrong with them?"

"Uh, hello! They're boys' sneakers, and they're way too big. I figured your family got them second-hand or something."

"Why don't you—"

"Girls! What are you doing up there? You're supposed to be lookouts. Whale blows, two o'clock!" Gus's irritated growl reverberated through the speakers.

Both of them jumped up and grabbed their binoculars. Sure enough, there were puffs of something off in the distance. Alex's pulse quickened. She was going to see Daredevil again!

Evania Rose seemed to fly over the waves. As they drew closer, Alex could make out dark forms in the water. Her heart sank. They weren't the same kind of whales as yesterday.

"It's a pod of minke whales! They're the littlest ones around here," Rachel said, still peering through the binoculars.

"Oh." Disappointed, Alex turned around to scan in the other direction.

"Hello! The whales are this way!"

Ignoring Rachel, Alex searched for her baby whale. Suddenly, a black form flashed in front of her lenses. Alex dropped the binoculars, grabbed the digital camera, and snapped as the whale dove beneath the surface.

"Alex, did you get that fluke?" Gus asked.

She checked the digital screen. It was a blur. She leaned towards the speaker and pushed the two-way button. "Nope."

"Bogs! That's what I thought. My eyes must be playing tricks, was sure it was Rooftop for a second, but didn't see her calf. Could've been Shuttle, I s'pose...she's never had a calf as far as we know. Or maybe it was

Lacuna, one of the males." Gus's musings echoed over the speaker.

They watched for a few more minutes, but the whale didn't return.

As they moved around the bay for the tour, they spotted several humpbacks, some with calves. But there was no sign of Daredevil and Rooftop.

Alex missed more whales than she caught on camera. Gus was calling them by name as he identified them—Sickle, Hopper, Cloud, and Peajack. They also saw Touchdown with a calf, Flash, Highlighter, Notchy, and Gremlin.

She was fascinated with it all, and made a game with herself of trying to find the distinguishing marks on their flukes that would have been the inspiration for their unique names.

But it was hard to watch and take pictures at the same time.

"Rats!" she muttered as she missed another. "There must be some other way to tell who these guys are besides their tails."

"They're called flukes, not tails," Rachel corrected. "And no, there isn't."

Alex gritted her teeth. *Evania Rose* sputtered to a stop as they approached the area where there had been whale blows a few minutes before. She scanned the water, waiting for one to appear.

"There she is!" Rachel's excited squeal pierced the air.

A humpback broke the surface briefly. Alex was getting used to their movements and could tell that the whale was preparing to go deep and that its tail should be visible any second. She focused the camera and caught it perfectly.

"That's Rooftop," Gus said.

Finally! Alex leaned over the railing, looking for Daredevil. Nothing. He must have gone under before they got there. She waited patiently for mom and baby to resurface, camera ready. Minutes passed. Her aunt's camera whirred, the zoom retracting as it went into standby mode.

Where are they? Alex wondered.

"Over there!" Rachel called, pointing off the right side of the bow.

Alex sprinted to the opposite railing. There was still only one whale. That couldn't be right.

More agitated by the second, Alex raced from one side of the boat to the other. Where was Daredevil? Maybe she needed to be down close to the water, like before, and he would come up to see her again.

She scurried to the metal railing and stepped out onto the first rung of the ladder to the lower deck. At the same moment, the engine roared to life and the boat jerked forward.

Alex stumbled. Her right foot slipped off the thin rubber grip of the rung and her sneaker sailed off her foot and through the air. She grabbed for the side railing, but her arm got tangled in the swinging camera strap.

"Look out!" Rachel screamed.

Alex swung her head back and her eyes locked with Rachel's panicked gaze for an instant before she plummeted to the deck below.

CHAPTER TEN

"SHE'S BEEN SLEEPING A LONG time," a voice whispered. "Is she okay?"

"The doctor said she didn't have any broken bones, but maybe a concussion. She was unconscious for over a minute. And then she seemed disoriented on the helicopter."

"Well, Gus said she hit her head pretty hard!"

"I can't...can't handle this again," a teary voice said. A voice Alex recognized.

"Mom," she croaked.

"Alexandra, thank god!"

A cool hand gripped hers. Alex slowly opened her eyes. Her mother's pale face hovered over her, her light blue eyes filled with tears.

"What are you doing here?" It was like a dream. She couldn't remember the last time her mother had actually looked directly at her. Maybe she *was* dreaming.

"Sophie called me. I was in Moncton visiting Lucy and Anna." She gestured towards her friends standing by the door. Her mom's voice shook. "When she said you'd hit your head...it was Adam all over again." Sobbing, she collapsed in the chair beside the bed, leaning her forehead against their jointly clasped hands.

Her mother's warm tears ran down the back of Alex's hand. Alex swallowed at the sudden tightness in her throat as she was transported back to all those days and nights in the hospital, keeping vigil by Adam's bedside. A sickly, familiar smell of antiseptic snaked up her nostrils, burning like acid. Instantly, nausea erupted from her stomach in a raging volcano.

Alex turned her head and threw up. Rolling over on her side, she clasped her midriff as she heaved again and again, continuing long past when there was anything left inside her. When the spasms stopped, she collapsed back against the pillows, gasping.

"It's okay, sweetheart." Her mom's quivering voice attempted to reassure her.

"Hey, kiddo," Aunt Sophie said. She reached over and placed a cool, damp cloth on Alex's forehead.

Alex sighed and closed her eyes. The throbbing under her lids eased. That was just what she used to do for Adam. Had it made him feel better too? She never knew.

"Am I in the hospital?" She didn't know why she asked. The smells had already told her where she was before she'd opened her eyes.

"Yes, in Halifax. We came by helicopter. Do you remember?" Aunt Sophie asked.

Images of blue sky and roaring engines flickered in her head. "Sort of, I guess. It's a little fuzzy."

"We were so worried." Her mom's voice cracked as she wiped her eyes with a tissue.

Alex leaned back against the pillows. "Can we leave?"

She had to get out of this place. She looked at her mother. "I'm okay, aren't I?"

"Well, I think you'll need to stay here overnight." Her mother seemed to regain some of her composure and smiled through her tears. "That was quite a smack, and you were unconscious for a while. Let's hear what the doctor has to say."

A while later, a man in a white coat entered the room. Alex watched him warily. He looked nice enough, but she didn't care much for doctors. They were at the top of her hate list, along with hospitals, big dogs, and cooked liver.

"Well, we've had a look at your scans and they're clear. But we'll keep you overnight for observation, just to be on the safe side."

"I thought you might," her mom sighed, nodding. "I know quite a bit about...head injuries."

"Is that so? Are you in the medical profession?"

Her mom and Sophie exchanged a long look.

"Not really," Aunt Sophie said.

The doctor glanced from her mom to Aunt Sophie again, waiting for an explanation. When none came, he shrugged and consulted his chart.

"The nurse will be in to check on her through the night and I'll be back in the morning," he said. "I suggest you get some rest, young lady."

A nurse came in and hustled everyone out a few minutes later, stating that the patient needed quiet and rest. Alex played along, making a production of blinking sleepily and yawning. Her mom's friends, Lucy and Anna, gave her a small wave and left.

Her mom whispered that she'd be back in a little while, and then she and Aunt Sophie quietly slipped out as well. Alex's gaze roamed around the empty room. She could still feel the imprint of her mom's kiss on her cheek.

She couldn't believe this was happening. It was like living a nightmare. And where was her dad? Why wasn't he here? Beads of sweat broke out on her forehead as a wave of panic suddenly overwhelmed her.

Here she was, back in the same hospital—the place she'd sworn she'd never return to. Not even if she broke every bone in her body. Not even if she was about to die.

CHAPTER ELEVEN

"WAKE UP, DEAR," A VOICE whispered.

Alex blinked, reluctantly leaving her dream behind. Only a trickle of a tear slid down her cheek this time. Usually, when she woke up from the dream, she was sobbing rivers of tears. Maybe she was finally running out of them.

"Sorry, I have to check on you every few hours," the nurse said softly. She held a finger to her lips and pointed to Alex's mom sleeping in the chair.

"It's okay." Alex could still hear Adam's whoop of excitement, but as if from a distance. The dream was always about Adam.

The nurse gave Alex a brief check-up, asked her a few questions, and then left.

Wide awake now, Alex sat up. Her head was aching and she reached up to touch the bandage on her forehead.

Her mom was still asleep in a chair by the bed. She had pulled a corner of Alex's blanket over her legs and put a rolled-up towel behind her head.

Her mom hadn't stirred during the nurse's visit. *She must be exhausted*, Alex thought as she slipped out of bed. The floor was icy cold on her bare feet. She draped more of the blanket over her mom, tucking it around her arms.

When she touched her hand, Alex noticed her mom's rings were almost slipping off her fingers. That was odd—she was always complaining they were too tight. Had she lost weight?

Alex crawled back on the bed, shoving her toes under the covers. She gazed around the room. It was frightening how much it was like the one Adam had been in. The only difference was that it had one window instead of two. Why were they all so ugly? They should each be different, with patterned curtains and brightly painted walls—cheerful. The blah surroundings only made you sicker, she was sure.

Curling in a ball, she closed her eyes, trying to block out the sights and sounds. She wished she could escape back to her and Adam's fun adventures, exploring the woods.

But her dreams never took her there.

It didn't matter how hard she tried before she went to sleep, concentrating on the woods, wishing she could dream of those days again and remember every detail. How fast could Adam climb a tree? She should know that.

She squeezed her eyes tighter. If she couldn't control her dreams, then she would search her memories—search for a perfect one. But her mind was not quick to obey, either. No, not the one of Adam scampering over a tower of rocks, while she painstakingly picked her way around them. Nor the one of him hopscotching on slippery stones across a swollen brook, while she trod carefully along the bank until she found a safe crossing on a sturdy fallen log.

No. No. No.

Then, as bright as its blue wings, the playful jay from last summer popped into her head. Alex had wanted to go to Shakespeare by the Sea, so her mom had dropped them off at Point Pleasant Park for the afternoon. Adam had agreed to go with her, but only after she promised she'd fork over her allowance for two weeks.

They were sitting by the Cambridge Battery before the show, eating their lunch. Adam had brought a bag of peanuts. Alex asked for one and he tossed it underhand to her. Out of nowhere, a blue blur swooped down and snatched it in mid-air.

Alex watched the blue jay land on a nearby tree branch. Thinking it had to be a one-time trick, she asked Adam to toss another. The blue jay again caught it in mid-air. They couldn't figure out what he did with all the peanuts, but time after time he'd catch them, until the bag was empty. They sat there under the warm summer sun, laughing until their sides ached.

A perfect memory, Alex thought, as she drifted off to sleep.

CHAPTER TWELVE

ALEX WOKE TO FIND HER mom already up. She looked agitated and was talking to herself. "It'll be all right," her mom said. "Everything will be all right." She was balanced on the edge of the chair, rocking back and forth.

"Mom, I feel fine."

Her mom stared at the wall.

"Mom!"

"What? Oh, sorry, honey. Yes, of course you're okay."

"Are you sure?" Alex watched her mom's clenched hands.

"The doctor should be here any minute."

The hospital room was stifling. Her mom obviously didn't feel like talking. Where was everyone? "How come Dad's not here?"

Her mom stiffened in the chair. "Oh, he's…away. We'll call him later, okay?"

Alex slumped back against the pillows. "Where did Aunt Soph go?"

"She's visiting one of her Brier Island neighbours whose son is in the cardiac unit. Mr. uh, R…something or other." Her mother went back to staring at the wall and kneading her hands.

Alex picked up a pen and a newspaper from the bedside table. In no time, she had completed all the word puzzles. Her hand automatically started doodling. She often made designs out of names.

Alex sketched a lion mane and a boat around Gus's name. Then she printed Eva's name and drew flowers around it. Eva...something tickled her brain. Eva...she looked at the boat around Gus's name again. Evania, she doodled. Wasn't that what Gus had named his boat? The *Evania Rose*? Could the similar names be a coincidence? Maybe.

The rest of the morning passed by so slowly, it was torture. Aunt Sophie returned around ten with coffees and juice. Alex got poked and prodded a few more times. Then they waited, and waited, and waited some more.

Finally, after twelve, the doctor returned and said she could leave. Other than the cut on her head, he pronounced her on the mend. "Now, just keep an eye on her, like I told you," he said to her mother. "If she shows any symptoms, bring her back in. Everything you need to know is in the pamphlet on concussions I gave you. But she should be fine."

Free at last, Alex sucked in a deep breath as she, her mom, and Aunt Sophie walked across the parking lot. The fresh air smelled extra sweet. As soon as she got in the back seat, she rolled the window down and rested her chin on the frame. Her stomach growled.

"Mom, can we get a donair at Pizza Corner?"

"Not a chance."

"C'mon, please?"

"That stuff will rot your stomach!"

"Aunt Sophie, help."

"Barkin' up the wrong tree here, kiddo." Aunt Sophie winked at Alex in the rearview mirror. "I'm with your mother on this one. Donair meat? Come on! I raise my own chickens, for Pete's sake."

"I was in the hospital. Don't I get, like, a mercy meal or something? I'm starving."

"For heaven's sake," her mom huffed.

But she looked like she was wavering. A guilt trip can be a beautiful thing. "Mom…" Alex whimpered.

"Oh, fine," her mom relented, "but only a small one."

Aunt Sophie scowled as she veered down Spring Garden Road. "This traffic is insane," she muttered, slamming on the brakes as a blue SUV cut in front of them.

"Bogs!" Alex yelled and waved her fist. "Watch where you're going!"

"Bogs?" her mom said. "What's that, some new kids' slang?"

"More like an old dog's slang," Aunt Sophie smirked. "I think my island's rubbing off on you, Alex."

Alex frowned. "Yeah, rubbing off like a virus," she muttered. She pictured Gus and Eva being shocked at her words and bit her lip. It didn't seem to matter what she did; guilt was never far behind.

Swearing again, this time at the lack of parking, Aunt Sophie dropped Alex's mom off and circled the block.

"I miss home," Aunt Sophie lamented as she leaned back against the headrest. Having given up on finding a legal parking spot, they were now double-parked in front of the pizza shop.

Alex watched the pedestrians scurrying along the sidewalks as they chatted into cell phones, at the same time balancing lattes and lugging briefcases. The women were the most amazing—some of them doing all those things while teetering on three-inch heels.

For some reason, she thought of Aunt Sophie's friend Henry, the old parchment-paper guy riding the museum bike on the quiet dusty road. Brier Island and Halifax— they were so different. It was hard to believe they were in the same country, let alone the same province.

"Do you ever miss the city? You know, shopping and movies?" Alex asked her aunt.

"Not even for a second."

Alex thought of Daredevil.

"Maybe you and your mom can come back with me."

"What about Dad?"

Aunt Sophie didn't answer, instead turning on the radio and then rooting through her bag.

"Did Mom talk to him?"

"I think she left him a message."

Her mom opened the door and eased into the front seat, balancing an enormous platter covered in aluminum foil.

"Jeez, Mom, that's humungous!"

"I know…I got in there and it smelled so good—"

Aunt Sophie's mouth was hanging open. "You didn't!"

"I did." Her mom giggled self-consciously. "I couldn't help it. I got an extra-large one…and three forks."

"Three forks? Don't drag me into this. You two are on your own." Aunt Sophie looked disgusted.

The hot, spicy smell of the donair filled the car. Alex's stomach rumbled louder. "Pass it back!"

"It'll get all over the seats. Soph, drive to Point Pleasant."

At the park, they walked past Black Rock Beach and onto the grass to a picnic table by the water. With the feast spread out in front of them, Alex and her mom loaded up their forks with the warm donair meat, pita bread, chopped tomatoes, and onions lathered in sauce.

Aunt Sophie apparently grew tired of the moans of pleasure and reached across the table to stab the smallest piece of meat. Wrinkling her nose, she nibbled it delicately. "Mmmm, not bad," she said, gulping down the rest in one bite.

It was a feeding frenzy.

Forks flew and mouths chomped. The gulls squawking nearby were out of luck. Within minutes, all that remained was a slab of soggy pita sitting in a puddle of sauce.

"I can't believe we just did that," her mom said. "I haven't had one of those since I was a teenager."

"It was my first," Aunt Sophie said, then burped. She slapped a hand over her mouth.

Her mom hooted. "Ha! Your first? You used to scarf them down too! Remember, back in the days before you got into all that organic stuff?"

"I don't recall—must have blocked it out," Aunt Sophie snickered.

The two sisters doubled over, their shoulders shaking with laughter.

Suddenly, the warm taste of the donair turned sour in Alex's mouth. It was wrong—wrong to be sitting here by the ocean like normal people, laughing in the sunshine.

"Donairs were Adam's favourite."

Her mother gasped and looked like she'd been slapped. Aunt Sophie's laughter broke off as if the mute button had been pushed on the remote.

Alex immediately regretted it. Why had she said that? It just popped out.

No one spoke.

The circling gulls' screams filled the silence.

Her mom eventually stood up and headed back the way they'd come. Without saying a word, Aunt Sophie picked up her bag and followed her.

Walking as slowly as possible to delay returning to the car, Alex stopped halfway to the parking lot and glanced back at where they had been sitting. Two gulls had landed on the picnic table. They were fighting over the pita bread, ripping it apart with their long, sharp beaks. The huge brown speckled one nipped at the other, making it drop the pita, then snatched up the bread in its beak. It took off, soaring over the trees.

Alex tilted her head back and watched until the gull had disappeared, then slowly made her way back to the car.

CHAPTER THIRTEEN

AFTER A SILENT RIDE HOME, Alex was the first out of the car, barely waiting for it to stop. She went upstairs. There was no way she could look at her mom right now.

Her room was the same dark tomb. The curtains were pulled tightly closed, like she had left them. It was the complete opposite to Aunt Sophie's airy, sunlit rooms. She pulled back one of the curtains, letting in a sliver of sunlight.

It didn't help. Alex stepped back out into the hall, her eyes drawn to Adam's door. Automatically, her feet padded along the corridor towards it.

Passing by her parents' room, she stopped. There were hushed voices coming from inside. Her dad must be home.

Alex grabbed the doorknob and was about to open it when she paused. Something wasn't right. Their voices sounded strange. She pressed her ear against the space along the frame.

"Douglas, what are you doing here? I thought we agreed—"

"I'm only picking up a few things."

"She's here!"

"What? I thought she was at your sister's for the month."

"Something happened. She's okay now, but—"

"What do you mean, she's okay now?"

Her dad's voice was getting louder. Alex winced—another fight.

"Watch the tone, Douglas. She had a little accident and hit her head. We ended up at the hospital overnight, but—"

"You should have called me, Colleen!"

No wonder Dad wasn't at the hospital. Mom didn't even call him! Alex couldn't believe it.

"I'm sorry, but I had other things on my mind, all right? Anyway, I thought you were in Toronto at your brother's."

Her mom's voice had risen too. Alex knew where this was going. They'd be yelling at the top of their lungs any second.

Alex knocked and turned the knob at the same time, stepping into the room. "Dad?"

Her mother and father were glaring at each other from opposite sides of the bed. Her dad was holding a shirt and there was an open suitcase on the bed.

"Munch, are you all right?" He grabbed her in a fierce hug. "I'm so sorry I wasn't there."

"Dad, you're squishing me!" Alex wiggled in the stranglehold. It was good to see him. She decided not to remind him, for the hundredth time, to stop using the munchkin nickname he'd called her since she was a baby.

"Sorry." He released Alex gently. "Your head..." He touched the bandage, inspecting her wound. "What happened?"

"Kind of a long story. But I'm okay, really." Alex gestured to the suitcase. "You never told me you were going to Uncle Raymond's."

Her dad glanced towards the doorway. "You heard that?"

"Yeah. How come you didn't take *me*?"

"It was a last-minute thing. Plans were already made for you to go to your aunt's, so..."

"That's right," her mom said.

Her dad tossed the now crumpled shirt on top of the pile in the suitcase.

"You're packing, not unpacking? Are you going away again?"

"Uh...I thought I'd do a Yarmouth run. I've missed so much time at work..."

Alex brightened. "Yarmouth? Then you can come back down to Aunt Sophie's with us tomorrow. It's on the way, right?"

"I have to work, sweetie. It's probably best if you both go back like you planned." Her dad avoided her gaze as he bent down to zip his suitcase closed.

"Dad, tomorrow's Saturday. You never work on the weekends." Alex plunked onto the bed. "You can come for the weekend and work on Monday."

Her dad stared down at her upturned face. Finally, he cracked the teeniest of smiles. "All right, Munch, if that's what you want."

"Douglas, I don't think—"

"It'll be fine, Colleen."

"Fine...yes, I'm sure." Her mother's lips were pressed tightly together.

As her parents stared wordlessly at each other, Alex felt a shiver run through her. Things didn't seem fine... not at all.

CHAPTER FOURTEEN

LATE IN THE NIGHT, ALEX woke from a restless sleep. Her alarm clock glowed two a.m. She felt uneasy, the remains of sleep still holding on to her.

Getting up, she roamed through the silent house. Adam's room was just as she had left it, too. It would have been a surprise if anything had changed. No one else went in there. Alex was careful to step over the squeaky board inside the doorway, preferring her late-night prowl to go undetected.

She sat at Adam's desk by the window and clicked on his computer. Waiting for it to boot up, her hand automatically searched the top drawer, pulling out one of the bags of sour candies she kept there.

Adam had set the computer to automatically sign in to one of his games. The first time she'd come in here after the accident, she'd noticed he was still logged on. There were pages of chat from gaming buddies all over the world. She'd watched it for a while, wondering what Adam used to say to them. Then, on an impulse, she'd replied to one of the blinking "Hey dude, what's up?" messages on the screen.

"Nothing," she'd replied to Gustavo from Chile.

"Adam, where ya been? Try that new move I told

you about?" Another chat buddy popped up. Taine from New Zealand.

"Not yet," Alex typed.

"Cool. Remember to flip from the tail…" And so it went.

Every night after that, Alex would come to Adam's room and chat with his online friends. They were from all over—Brazil, Germany, Australia. There was some guy at a research station in Antarctica, another working at a diamond mine far up in the North. They never suspected it wasn't Adam chatting with them. Why would they? None of them were local, so they wouldn't know what had happened.

For some reason, it had made her feel…connected to him, or something. In a weird way, it was as if she was talking to him, like people did when they visited the graves of their loved ones. Only she never went to Adam's grave. She tried once, but couldn't go through with it.

Tonight, she watched the chatter back and forth, but didn't feel like joining in. Instead, on a whim, she searched "Brier Island whales." Gus's site came up first. She clicked on it and started reading the blog. There was a bunch of entries from this summer already. She saw a few mentioning Rooftop with her calf, Gus talking about the new boat, the count of how many calves had been spotted so far, along with all the humpbacks identified.

She clicked on another whale watch site for the area— it had a similar daily blog. She read the entry for that day and sighed with relief. Rooftop had been sighted with her calf. So Daredevil was all right after all. It must be like Gus said—he just strayed from his mother now and then.

Alex realized she was looking forward to seeing Eva and Gus, and especially Daredevil. Her day had been so bizarre, even Rachel didn't seem so bad now. Alex flicked off the computer monitor. As she was returning the open bag of candies to the drawer, a few fell. She reached under the desk to get them and noticed her brother's pack on the floor.

Alex looked through the compartments. Adam's Swiss Army pocket knife was tucked in the front pouch. Dad had given it to him on Alex and Adam's twelfth birthday. She had wanted one too, but got a new easel instead. She tucked the knife into her pyjama pocket.

There was also a half-filled bottle of iced tea and a partially eaten granola bar. She smiled for just a second—Adam always had food with him wherever he went.

She dropped the knife off in her room, then went downstairs. She tiptoed past the family room, where her dad was slumped sideways, asleep on the couch in front of the television. That seemed to be his bed these days.

"For just $39.95 and from the comfort of your chair, you'll have rock hard abs in no time!" a voice blared from an infomercial.

In the kitchen, she fished an ice cream sandwich out of the freezer, and continued her nighttime prowl. Aunt Sophie was sleeping in the office on the hide-a-bed. The door was closed, but Alex could clearly hear her rattling snore in the hallway. She'd gotten used to it at her aunt's place on Brier Island. It amazed her that such a big sound could come out of such a tiny person.

Opening the patio blind, she gazed out into the backyard. Light reflected on the surface of their in-ground pool. No one had put the solar blanket on. Alex punched in the code to deactivate the alarm, flicked on the switch for the underwater lights, and slipped quietly outside.

She sat down by the stairs going into the pool. A drip of melting ice cream splashed on the water. Alex quickly took another bite of the sandwich and licked the drippy parts. Her head was throbbing. She felt the bandage, her fingers running over the big goose egg on her forehead.

Leaves and twigs bobbed on the pool surface. The automatic pool cleaner was meandering along the bottom.

Adam and his friends used to swim almost every day in the summer. Ghostly images of bathing-suit-clad boys and girls splashed and shimmered in front of her as she continued to nibble her ice cream.

Adam was scrambling up the ladder and running as fast as he could down the board.

"Cannonball!" he bellowed, crashing into the water and sending a tidal wave over everyone.

"Nice one, man!" his friend Mark yelled.

"Oooh, Adam, you soaked my new bikini!" Chelsea, the boy-crazy girl from next door, squealed.

Alex remembered grumbling as she brushed water drops off her book, telling them to stop messing around.

Sighing, she gazed up at the diving board. Adam had tried to entice her up there a million times. She never had gone. Not once. No wonder he called her a wuss. Alex took a deep breath and slipped her toes into the water. It was cool. On impulse, she slid into the pool. The water came up to her waist. The legs of her pyjama shorts billowed out around her like two little umbrellas.

She slid her feet along the bottom towards the drop-off. Adam used to try to trick her into going over when they were younger. But it didn't matter what games they played, she always instinctively knew where the drop-off started and would turn back before going over it.

Alex had never lost that uneasiness in the water. Not like Adam. Of course, he swam like a fish. She had managed to learn a puttering form of the dog paddle, but still remained scared of deeper water. According to Adam, that wasn't really swimming.

Her toes felt the downward slope of the concrete. She gulped, tightening her grip on the pool edge. Her heart raced as she gazed up at the high diving board. What would it be like to climb up there?

Suddenly, her foot slipped and she was sliding into deeper water. Waves lapped at her chin. She tried to gain traction on the concrete bottom, grasping the side of the pool.

Gripping the edge, Alex quickly returned to the stairs and stepped out of the pool. Her sopping bottoms fell down past her waist to the ground. She kicked them off and flopped into one of the loungers.

Her head was throbbing worse than ever. Leaning back on the cushion, she closed her eyes. Why had she panicked like that? She hadn't even tried to swim.

Why was she always so afraid of everything?

CHAPTER FIFTEEN

"YOU'RE NOT TAKING THOSE SHOES."

"I have to—they're my only ones."

"Alexandra, these are your brother's skateboarding shoes." Her father scooped them up off the floor. "Where are your sneakers?"

"I can't find them."

"Well, time to look again. These," he said, tucking them on the top shelf of the hall closet, "are staying here."

"But—"

"No buts. Sophie said you tripped in the blasted things and that's why you fell. They're too big for you!"

"But I like them…" Alex's voice trailed off as she stared up at the backs of Adam's skate shoes.

Her father sighed. He wrapped his arm around her shoulders. "I know you do. But I don't want you hurting yourself. I'm sorry. You'll have to stick to your own from now on, okay?"

"Sure, Dad."

"That's it?" Her father looked surprised. "No arguments?"

"Would you change your mind?"

"Well, no."

Alex shrugged and went up to her room.

What she didn't tell her father was that she hadn't looked all that hard for her own. After a few pokes at the clothes piles in her closet, she found them. Slipping her feet into the snug sneaks, she tightened the laces. It felt good to wear shoes that fit.

Adam had always been bigger than her, even when they were born. His shoes were too big. At first, wearing them had made her feel as if he was close by—like he had just kicked them off and if she turned the corner, she'd see him eating out of the fridge, or see him sprawled across the couch watching TV.

Lately, it hadn't been like that—just her tripping everywhere she went. But she'd felt disloyal at the thought of not wearing them. Even now, part of her wanted to sneak downstairs and get them back. But she didn't.

Alex grabbed her pack off the bed and took one last look around her gloomy room. Walking over to the window, she pulled the curtains wide open. Sunlight beamed in, lighting up the dark space. *That's better*, she thought. She strolled out, leaving the bedroom door open this time.

"I think you and I should go with Sophie. She needs the company. It'll be fun—the girls' car."

"No way, Mom," Alex cried. "The three of us have to go together—you, me, and Dad. Aunt Sophie can come in our car too, if she wants. She can leave her car here."

Alex and her mom were standing in the kitchen by the door to the garage. Her dad was loading the luggage into the trunk.

"Your father needs his car for work, so we have to take both cars."

"She'll be okay. Won't you, Aunt Sophie?"

Aunt Sophie was just coming through the doorway into the kitchen. "Okay with what?"

"Driving in your car by yourself."

Aunt Sophie raised her eyebrows as she glanced over at Alex's mom. "Hmm, both of you are going with Douglas?"

"Apparently."

"That should be interesting," Aunt Sophie said.

"Knock it off, Soph."

"Right, sis."

"What are you guys talking about?"

"Never mind, Alex. It's fine. We'll go together." Her mother looped her purse over her shoulder. "We should get going."

"It's only 8:30. What's the rush?" Aunt Sophie held up the empty carafe. "No coffee?"

"Hit the drive-through on the way," Alex's mom said.

"Drive-through?" Aunt Sophie shuddered. "I really miss my island. One of Eva's warm ham and cheese rolls and a piping hot cinnamon coffee would sure hit the spot."

"You'll have to suffer. Alex, you can sit up front with your father. I'm going to read."

"Really, I can have the front seat?" Alex said.

"Absolutely." Her dad smiled at her mom. Only it was a hard smile, like he gave to Frank the Crank, the neighbour none of them liked. Then he slammed the trunk so hard, the car shook.

Her mom and Aunt Sophie exchanged glances before going outside.

Both cars were soon on the 101 highway, heading towards Windsor—and Brier Island.

"Mom, how come you didn't go to Toronto with Dad?"

"What, dear?"

Alex turned sideways in her seat, so she could look at both her parents.

"Toronto—how come *you* didn't go?"

Her mom was staring at the back of her dad's head, as if waiting for him to say something. He didn't. "The flights were too expensive."

"I thought Dad had, like, a gazillion frequent-flyer miles from his last job?"

Her dad didn't answer. With his eyes hidden behind wraparound sunglasses he looked like a statue.

"Dad?"

"Good grief, enough with the twenty questions. Your dad just wanted to visit his brother—end of story!" Her mother huffed and opened her book.

Alex looked from one silent, stone-faced parent to the other. "Well, this was a great idea," she mumbled. "I should have gone with Aunt Sophie!" Putting on her headphones, she cranked her MP3 player.

So much for family time.

CHAPTER SIXTEEN

THE DRIVE ONLY GOT WORSE after that. Alex tried to start conversations, but the grumbled one-word answers, if she got any at all, weren't worth the trouble. At least when they stopped for lunch, she had Aunt Sophie to talk to.

Strolling down Digby's main street, Alex saw scallops on the specials board of a café. "Let's go in here!"

Alex raced ahead through the dark interior and picked a table on the balcony overlooking the harbour. Everyone settled into the rattan chairs and ordered iced teas. A sailboat whizzed along close to shore, on its way to deeper water. Its bright red and yellow sails billowed full in the breeze.

"Scallop Days are a lot of fun here. You should come for that sometime," Aunt Sophie said.

Neither of her parents responded. Alex felt like she had to say something. "Sounds like fun," she muttered lamely.

"We have a big bike rally here in September. It's quite a sight, motorcycles everywhere you look."

Alex could tell Aunt Sophie was trying to make things more comfortable. Her mom was staring off in one direction, her dad another.

Alex scanned the menu. There were some odd things on there—Solomon Gundy, dulse, Digby chicks?

"Ready to order there, hon?" The waitress smiled at her.

"Um, what are Digby chicks?" Alex wrinkled her nose. Who would eat little baby chicks? Gross.

The waitress laughed. "It's not what you think. They're smoked herring."

"Herring?"

"Early settlers couldn't afford poultry. Renaming the herring must've made it sound better." The waitress shrugged.

"Ick! It would still taste the same." Alex shook her head. "No chicks for me."

Aunt Sophie and her mom chuckled. Even her dad cracked a smile. It broke the solemn mood for a bit. Their meals came and they passed around the tartar sauce and ketchup, raving about how good the food was. It was nice.

Afterward, Alex and her aunt strolled along the boardwalk. Her dad was making calls on his cell phone and her mom had gone into a craft shop. Alex was in temporary food heaven, slurping a triple-decker butterscotch ripple ice cream. Aunt Sophie had a maple walnut.

Alex felt almost bouncy in her sneakers—especially not having to curl her toes like she did in Adam's shoes to keep them from falling off. No toe cramps.

All kinds of boats were tied up at the wharf. The coolest were the fishing boats. Some had long horizontal arms and rigging that looked like angel wings as they bobbed back and forth on the choppy waves. The wind blew in off the water. Alex tucked her dark, wavy hair behind her ears to keep it from whipping around her face.

She gazed out at the water, troubling thoughts looming inside her head. "Aunt Soph, what's the matter with my parents? You and Mom talk all the time. You know, right?"

Her aunt's footsteps slowed. "What do you mean?"

"They're always fighting."

"Well, adults argue from time to time."

"I'm not a kid—I know grown-ups fight," Alex said. She thought of the mean words and looks that seemed to be her parents' only interactions lately. "But this is different. Ever since…Adam…they talk to each other like Craig and I do. He's a guy in my school—and we don't like each other one bit."

"Well, they're having a tough time too, you know."

"I guess."

"They miss your brother—just like you do. And they're very sad, and angry too, that he's gone."

Alex sat down on a bench facing the harbour. "I know they're sad. But why do they have to fight?" She didn't know why she was bothering to ask the question. She knew why her parents were fighting. It was because of her, because of what she did.

"It's hard for everyone, Alex."

Alex looked up into her aunt's blue eyes, searching for the blame that should be there. Her aunt must think it was her fault too, right? "Do you think it'll be okay, Aunt Soph?"

"I hope so, kiddo. I sure hope so."

Aunt Sophie sat down beside Alex. They stared at the waves in silence as they finished their ice cream cones, waiting for Alex's parents to join them.

It turned out that her dad had to go see a client, so they roamed the town for most of the afternoon. Alex didn't mind, although she was pretty tired. But her mom was complaining to Aunt Sophie that this was typical, and why couldn't he have told them beforehand. When her dad finally met up with them, it was almost suppertime and plans had changed.

"I have to drop by to see another client. It could take a while, so you should go down with Sophie and I'll meet you there." Her dad popped the trunk and began transferring the bags to the other car.

"Really, Douglas?" Her mom was tapping her foot on the pavement. "More calls? On a Saturday?"

"Look, Colleen, I told you. I missed a lot of time. I need the calls when I can get them right now."

"It's okay, Dad," Alex jumped in. Her stomach was churning as her parents' voices rose. "We'll go with Aunt Sophie!" She wrapped her arms around her father's waist and hugged him tight. *Please don't fight. Please don't fight*, she repeated in her head.

He was stiff as a board for a minute. Then Alex felt him relax as he hugged her back. "Love you, Munch," he whispered. His voice sounded raspy. "See you tonight."

She looked up at him, but couldn't see his eyes behind his dark glasses. He seemed to be watching her mom. He stood there for another minute before getting into his car. Gravel flew as he sped out of the parking lot.

Aunt Sophie squeezed Alex's shoulder before sliding into the driver's seat of her car.

It wasn't until they were boarding the second ferry, the one at Freeport on Long Island that took them to Brier Island, that Alex's gloom lifted slightly. The car tilted forward as they descended the steep bank. The last time they had driven onto the ferry, it had been almost even with the road. The tide seemed to be all the way out today.

She hopped out of the car. The cool air was a shock, a big difference in temperature from Digby. Leaning against the metal railing, Alex found herself face to face with a wall of periwinkle shells and the seaweed her aunt called bladder wrack clinging to the wooden dock. She looked up—way up.

"Impressive, huh?" Aunt Sophie said. "The difference between high and low tide here is almost twenty feet. Highest tides in the world. That's a lot of water every six hours."

Alex nodded, remembering the tall stilts of the garage buildings covered with barnacles and seaweed.

"It'll be good to get back, huh, kiddo?" Aunt Sophie sighed.

Alex's gaze drifted to the village of Westport on the other side of the passage. She squinted, imagining she could see Eva's café. The lodge was clearly visible, high on the cliff.

"I was talking to Eva last night. She and Gus have been worried sick about you. It would be nice if we could pop in there first. Are you feeling up to it?" Aunt Sophie brushed her fingertips lightly against Alex's hair. "It's been a long day."

"We can go. I'm okay." Alex didn't mention the headache that was pulsing behind her eyes. But she didn't want to go back to Aunt Sophie's right away. She knew that as soon as her dad arrived her parents would probably start arguing again. "Where's Mom?"

"She stayed in the car."

The engine roared and they began to pull away from the dock. Alex tilted her face into the wind. They'd barely cleared the end of the wharf when Alex noticed dark forms in the water.

They were back in the other world that was Brier Island. The world of whales.

CHAPTER SEVENTEEN

"ALEX, LOOK," AUNT SOPHIE SQUEALED. "C'mon!"
She dragged Alex with her to the very front of the ferry.

Is Daredevil there? Alex peered over the side.

"Darn it. I need to get my camera."

Alex watched, amazed, as three whales breached high in the air before crashing back into the water. The ocean churned as more whales jumped and splashed. They were everywhere.

She couldn't take her eyes off the unbelievable scene.

The whirring and clicking of a camera told her Aunt Sophie had returned.

"What's all the fuss?" her mom asked. "Soph, you drag me out of the car for—what on earth?"

"I know, right?" Aunt Sophie cried.

"Look, there's another one!" someone called out.

"Two more behind us!"

Suddenly, the ferry slowed and the rumble of the engine ceased.

The captain's voice echoed over the speaker. "Seems like our whale friends have followed a school of herring here into Grand Passage."

Sure enough, Alex stared at the water and could see swirls of tiny fish beneath the surface. Just then, one of the humpbacks surged up under the fish, its jaw suddenly clamping shut around them.

"Wow!"

The gigantic creatures were in a feeding frenzy. They splashed, smacked their flippers, shot up in the air—Alex didn't know where to look. There was no way to tell if Rooftop and Daredevil were in the mix.

Everyone was out of their cars now, crowding around the railings and snapping pictures. They stayed like that, drifting in the current, until the frenzied pod continued away from them, on through the passage and out of sight.

"Welcome back to Brier Island," Aunt Sophie said. "I didn't plan this welcoming committee, I swear."

Alex managed a nod, but was disappointed not to have been able to tell if she'd seen Daredevil. As they drove off the ferry, another unexpected sight was waiting for them. Gus.

He was standing by his truck, waving like a nut. Aunt Sophie pulled up beside him and stuck her head out the window. "Hi, Gus. How did you know we were on this one?"

Gus leaned against the roof of their car and peered down at them. "Jimmy, the ferry captain, called me when you boarded."

In case she hadn't noticed already, this was proof for Alex that she was back in the land where everybody knew everybody. She squirmed, uncomfortable. Just when she'd rather hide away, unnoticed, she felt like an ant under a microscope.

"Have you seen Rooftop's baby since I left?" Alex blurted. "I saw on one of the blogs that he was around."

"As a matter of fact, I saw the little tyke yesterday on the afternoon tour. Not to worry. He's a wanderer all right, but he always ends up back safe with his mum," Gus said.

"I wasn't worried," Alex mumbled.

"Uh-huh. No matter, glad to have you all back safe and sound."

"We're going over to Eva's," Aunt Soph said.

"She was hoping ya would—made something special." Gus winked.

"Sis? I need to run up to the house for a minute," Alex's mom said. "I'll come down later."

"Oh, okay then." Aunt Sophie opened the car door. "Take the car. We can go with Gus. Or walk. It's only down the street."

Alex opened her door. But before she could get her foot down, Gus had swooped in and scooped her up in his arms.

"Gus, I can walk! I'm fine." She pushed her hands against his tree-trunk arms.

"Bogs! S'pose that bandage on your head is just for dress-up, eh?" he muttered gruffly.

Gus bounded across the gravel as if she weighed nothing and tucked her into the passenger seat of his pickup truck.

"Be right back—have to speak to your mum."

His long stride took him quickly back to where her mom was standing. He towered above her and Aunt Sophie, his bushy mane of hair blowing in the breeze. Alex thought he looked more like a lion than ever.

"Pleased to meetcha!" Gus extended his plate-sized hand towards her mom.

Her mother stood with her arms crossed in front of her. She made no move to take his hand and stared up at him. "Gus, the boat captain? The adult who was supposedly supervising my daughter when she almost got killed?"

Alex could hear the anger in her mom's voice. "Mom!"

"Uh, well, yes, she was on my boat." Gus's hand dropped back to his side. "I'm very sorry, ma'am. I feel awful about what happened…"

"Colleen, what are you doing?" Aunt Sophie sounded horrified. "You know it was an accident!"

"I have to go," her mom said, turning away and getting into the driver's seat. All of them watched her drive away.

"Gus, I don't know what came over her. She knows it wasn't your fault," Aunt Sophie said. "She's dealing with a lot of things and—"

"No, no, she's right. I shouldn't have let them go up on top alone—wasn't thinkin'." Gus's head slumped low as they made their way back to Alex and the truck. "Not used to looking after young ones, I guess."

Alex's stomach lurched. "No one pushed me or anything. My shoes—I slipped."

"It's all right there, Alex, not to worry." Gus gave her a weak smile and sighed. "Gave us a right fright. Yes indeed." He folded himself up in the driver's seat. It looked like it was back as far as it would go and his knees were still practically banging on the steering wheel.

No one spoke for the short ride down the street. When they entered the café, the smells of cinnamon and fresh bread tickled Alex's nose as the hummingbird wind chimes tinkled their greeting.

"Eva?" Sophie called.

"Well, there she is!" Eva bustled out from the back room and pulled Alex into her arms. It was like getting hugged by a pillow—a soft, squishy pillow that smelled like vanilla.

Alex murmured a weak protest into Eva's shoulder, but was ignored.

"Sweetie, so good to have you back!" Finally releasing her, Eva dabbed her watery eyes with a corner of her apron. "Heavens, look at me—blubbering like an old fool."

"Eva, it smells so good in here." Aunt Sophie plunked down on a stool. "I missed my island."

"Missed my food is more like it." Eva's eyes twinkled. "And no wonder—they don't know how to feed you on the mainland."

Aunt Sophie groaned as she took a huge drink from her coffee mug. "Oh yeah, that's the stuff—just like a blood transfusion."

She was fast. Alex hadn't even seen her go near the coffee pot.

"Sit down now, the rest of you. Hope you're hungry. I whipped up a special batch of my seafood chowder and buttermilk biscuits."

Eva bustled like a whirlwind around them, setting out

utensils, napkins, bowls of steaming chowder, and a platter of biscuits.

Gus quietly pulled a stool over and dug into his piled-high bowl. "Ya outdone yourself, Eva," he murmured politely, his mouth full.

Eva beamed as she circled around, refilling water glasses and dumping more biscuits on the platter.

"The chowder's wonderful! I know you've got some secret ingredient," Aunt Sophie said.

"Well, as a matter of fact, there is a little trick I've been using. I boil up a pot of fresh periwinkles. Now they're a bit too chewy for my taste, so I don't leave them in. But the broth makes a tasty base for my chowder."

"I knew there was something!"

They settled back after eating refilled bowls of chowder and countless biscuits. Alex moaned and held her stomach. After the big lunch they'd had in Digby, her insides felt stretched and ready to burst.

The steady stream of food and conversation seemed to have slowly brought Gus out from under his gloomy cloud. Finally, during dessert, he let out one of his roaring belly laughs.

Alex got a lump in her throat as she watched him gulp from his mammoth mug of tea, thinking of her own family dinners since Alex had died. They hardly ever ate together. When they did, no one laughed, that was for sure.

Eva had just started to talk about her garden and the new herbs she was using in her cooking, when Gus banged his mug on the table.

"I almost forgot," he said. Jumping up, he walked out the door to his pickup parked next to the café. Alex watched him open the big storage box in the bed of the truck and pull out a bouquet of flowers.

Cut flowers—ugh! Alex hated them. Flowers were supposed to stay attached to the rest of their bodies, growing in the ground, not be hacked up to die. They had been a constant presence in Adam's hospital room. Her mother had always replaced the drooping and dying ones with new ones—their overpowering perfumes mixing into a sickly sweet stench.

Her stomach rolled at the memory, chowder sloshing around inside her. She felt dizzy. Oh no, she knew that feeling. Any second now she was going to throw up.

CHAPTER EIGHTEEN

GUS STOOD IN THE MIDDLE of the room, holding the flowers awkwardly in front of him.

"They're, um, pretty," Alex managed to say, concentrating with all her might on not woofing her cookies all over the table. She sucked in a deep breath—thank goodness she couldn't smell them. *Look at something else!* she ordered herself. Staring at the tabletop, she felt the waves of nausea subside.

"I'd have been skinned alive if I'd forgotten 'em."

"They're not from you?" Alex asked.

"Nope. Not that I wouldn't have," Gus said. "But Rachel beat me to it. All tore up that you were hurt, she was. Ran off and picked these herself." He examined the blooms. "Now, I'm no expert like Soph, but I'd bet a whole lobster catch that there's some stuff in here that shouldn't be."

"Really?" Aunt Sophie said. "Like what?"

"Yup, some of Eva's prized dahlias, I believe," he said, gently tapping a burnt-orange bloom. "Should know—I weeded them myself."

"Uh-oh." As annoying as Rachel was, Alex didn't want her to get in any trouble.

"Don't worry, now. Eva couldn't yell if her life depended on it." His eyes crinkled at the corners. "Besides, can't blame Rachel for being so upset. We were all worried about ya…"

"Of course I don't mind." Eva got up and inspected the blooms. "Good taste, indeed. These are my favourites."

"Looks like little Rachel was in Big Meadow in the nature preserve and plucked a few endangered Eastern Mountain Avens while she was at it," Aunt Sophie grumbled, peering over Eva's shoulder.

"Ahem. Well, innocent mistake." Gus pulled the bouquet away from Aunt Sophie's inspection. He tucked it into an empty ceramic vase on the counter before returning to his tea. "Heart's in the right place, that's the important thing. Besides, flowers grow back. No harm done."

Silence settled on the group as each dug into their dessert and coffee refills. With the imminent threat of barfing now gone, Alex contemplated the juicy butter tart sitting in front of her.

Underneath the plate was a touristy placemat, covered with ads and little stories about the island. The writing on the paper mat twigged her memory of name doodling the previous day. She thought about Gus's boat, *Evania Rose*. "Eva, where does your name come from? I mean, is Eva your whole name?"

"What do you mean, dear?"

"You know, is it short for anything, like—uh, Evangeline? Or maybe something else?"

Eva looked at Alex curiously. "As a matter of fact, it is. My full name is Evania. What makes you ask?"

Alex glanced sideways at Gus. She could see a wave of red rising from his neck. His head was bent over his mug and he made a funny noise in his throat. She was definitely on to something.

"Really? That's an unusual name—very interesting," Alex said.

"Is it now?" Eva seemed puzzled.

"Have you ever been on Gus's new boat?" Alex sat forward on her stool.

"Not one toe—I get seasick something fierce. But what's that got to do with—"

"Ahem. Yes, well, it's getting late. Time to close up there, Eva?" Gus leapt to his feet and began grabbing plates off the table.

"Augustus Emmanuel, what on earth are you doing?" Eva looked flabbergasted. "You've never touched a dish here in all the twenty years I've known you."

Gus's face flamed brighter as he froze, his hand hovering over Eva's chowder bowl.

"Besides, I'm not even finished my dessert yet," Alex said. She took a tiny nibble of her tart, watching Gus. Part of her felt good that it was someone else on the squirmy end of a hook for a change.

"Bogs!" Gus growled, his ferocious lion scowl focused on her. "Cheeky girl."

"Don't be foolish. Sit down," Eva ordered, waving him back to his stool. She tipped his travel mug towards her and peered inside. "You haven't even finished your second cup of tea, for heaven's sake!"

"Bogs," he muttered again, so low it was hard to hear him. However, he obediently returned to his seat and piled the dishes in a precarious tower in the middle of the table, all the while sneaking glances at Eva.

"You were saying, Alex dear…"

Gus twitched and his bushy eyebrows sunk even lower as his gaze zigzagged between Eva and Alex.

Part of Alex knew it was none of her business—that she should leave it alone. But if Gus had a crush on Eva, he should just tell her. What was he waiting for, anyway? She didn't know why it even mattered to her, but at that moment it mattered a lot. "It's a very strange coincidence. Gus's boat's name—"

Crash!

The teetering stack of dishes toppled over. Two chowder bowls and a glass rolled off the edge of the table and smashed.

"My new stoneware!" Eva cried as she leapt up to grab one of the remaining bowls before it hit the floor.

Everyone scrambled into action, collecting dishes and pieces of the broken bowls while Eva tut-tutted her distress.

"It's my fault, Eva," Gus said. He was sprawled on his hands and knees, carefully checking under the table for broken pieces. "I'll get more bowls for ya."

"Don't be silly! It was an accident." Eva was trying to piece together one of the bowls. "I wonder if I can glue this…"

They'd just swept up the last shards of pottery when lights from outside lit up the café's interior. Alex's mom had pulled into the parking lot. She turned the car off, but didn't get out.

Aunt Sophie frowned and walked towards the door. "Be right back."

Alex watched as Aunt Sophie leaned in through the car window and said something. Then she opened the passenger door and got in. She was talking to Alex's mom and suddenly reached over and hugged her. They sat there, making no move to come in, and continued talking. What was happening? Alex was sure she knew the answer to that—*more trouble between Mom and Dad.*

Anxiety surged through her. She thought about finding out what was wrong, but decided she didn't want to know. Desperate to think of something else, Alex turned back to Eva and Gus.

"Gus named his boat after you!" she shouted.

CHAPTER NINETEEN

"WHAT?" EVA'S MOUTH WAS SHAPED in an O and her eyebrows had jumped almost to the top of her head.

"*Evania Rose*—that's what Gus named his new boat."

Gus slunk even lower on his stool. It looked like he was trying to melt into the floor. He shot Alex a hurt look.

She felt like she'd kicked a puppy. He suddenly didn't look the least bit like a ferocious lion. Why had she said anything? It was the same as at the park with the donair. Part of her wanted to ruin everything.

"What?" Eva repeated. "You named your boat…after me?"

Gus opened his mouth, but nothing came out.

"All these years, you never said a word."

"I—I, well, you were in mourning after Albert died… and—"

"Albert? He died ten years ago!"

"Yes, but ya love him—and miss him. I know that."

Eva was shaking her head. "You should have said something. All this time…"

He took both her hands. "Eva, dear. I'm a grimy old bachelor. And still, I weed your flowers, plant your fancy herbs, take you shopping on the mainland…"

"Yes, I know that, but—oh. Oh!" Her eyes were round as saucers as she looked up at him.

Gus smiled back down at her.

Eva seemed to get embarrassed. She tugged her hands loose. "What do you mean, grimy? Indeed you're not! You have the cleanest hands I've ever seen."

"There's a bit of a story behind that. Do you remember me coming in here one day after scrubbing down the boat? Must be five years ago now. I'd been working with bleach all day. My nails were cleaner than they ever were in my life. I was payin' for my coffee and you said, 'My, you have lovely hands, Gus. Why can't all men keep their nails like you?' Well, I been scrubbin' like a demon ever since."

"You bleach your hands? For me?"

"I did. But I had to switch to lemon juice. Bleach is a little hard on the skin—even my tough old hide."

So that explained his hands. Alex had noticed his perfect white nails the first time he shook her hand.

"Crazy old fool!" Eva blubbered. "I—I've got to get the dishes done here."

Gus's face fell. He took a step towards Eva and stopped, his hands dropping to his sides.

Just then, Aunt Sophie and Alex's mom entered the café. They were walking slowly and whispering, their heads bent towards each other. Aunt Sophie's arm was looped through her mom's. They didn't look anything alike, but when they were side by side, you could tell they were sisters. They walked exactly the same way.

Her mom's eyes were red and swollen, like she'd been crying again.

"What's the matter, Mom?"

"Nothing, Alex." Her mom's face quickly rearranged itself into a smile. "Just sister talk."

Sophie gave her mom another one of her long, stern looks before plucking the bouquet from the counter. She frowned into the blooms, then shrugged and tucked them into the crook of her arm. "Ready to go, kiddo?"

Alex was grateful that neither her aunt nor her mom noticed the weird way Eva and Gus were behaving. Now they weren't even looking at each other as Gus muttered awkward good nights to them. Eva simply waved from behind the counter, not turning around.

It was dark when they went outside. The moon glittered on the rippling waves of the harbour and the ferry's lights shone brightly as it sped across the passage. Alex was stuffed. She imagined Eva's tea biscuits as little boats in her stomach, floating on the ocean of seafood chowder she had eaten. After the disaster she'd caused with Gus and Eva, it felt like the cream had all curdled inside her—a big ball of sourness.

"I don't think I'll eat again for a year," Aunt Sophie moaned. "I lost count of how many biscuits I ate—couldn't resist. They were calling to me."

"Then they were callin' to all of us," Gus said from behind them.

Alex could feel her mom stiffen beside her. Gus put a light hand on Alex's shoulder, gently swinging her around.

He smiled down at her. "Owe you a debt, Alex, yes indeed," he murmured. "And I don't forget 'em, either. Not ever."

Gus thinks I was trying to do something good? she thought. Shame burned Alex's cheeks. She was glad for the darkness. "But she doesn't seem happy…"

"Bit of a shock is all. Should have said somethin' years ago. She'll come around." He gave them all a brief salute before climbing into his truck. Alex could still hear him whistling as he drove away down the street.

He was happy! Alex thought of all her own tears lately. Looking up at the ones still glistening in the moonlight on her mom's cheeks, she pictured her dad's face—an unsmiling stone mask hiding behind dark glasses.

Well, whatever the reason, at least someone was happy.

CHAPTER TWENTY

"I THOUGHT YOU HATED SKATEBOARDING," Adam said. His head was bent low over his board as he adjusted the wheels.

"I do. I mean, I did."

"So, why do you want to go?"

"That's all you do now. We never go exploring anymore."

"This is more fun," he said. "All you did was draw flowers and stuff while I climbed trees by myself."

"I did that too!"

"Ha! Only if I pulled you up the tree," he laughed.

"Stop teasing me!" Alex frowned.

"Sorry. You can go, okay?"

"Okay."

"But you're not gonna like it," he muttered, expertly flipping his board upright. "Skateboarding is higher on the scare-o-meter than climbing trees. Higher than roller coasters, too."

Alex gulped.

At the Halifax Commons skatepark, she watched in awe as Adam did amazing tricks, each higher and faster than the last. He really was fearless, she thought.

"All right, sis, you're up."

"Give me your helmet!"

He laughed and handed it over. She pulled the strap on the helmet as tight as it would go. Everyone was watching her.

"Get on and I'll push you around a bit so you can get used to the feel of it."

"Okay."

Alex stared at the skateboard. She willed her feet to move. They didn't. Seconds, then minutes, ticked by. The others got tired and returned to their boards, flying around her.

"C'mon, sis, you can do it. Don't be scared. I'm right here."

"All right, all right, don't rush me!" Alex put her right foot on the back end of the skateboard and shifted her weight to that same foot, like she was stepping onto a stair.

"Not on the tail—"

"Ahh!"

The skateboard flipped up and Alex lost her balance. She would have been sprawled on the pavement if Adam hadn't grabbed her.

"Gotcha!"

Laughter erupted around her. She felt her face flush.

"It's all right," he whispered in her ear. "Ignore them. I'll teach you when no one's around to tease you, okay? Watch, I'll show them a new trick. Then they'll forget all about laughing at you."

He grabbed the board and zipped off.

"Wait, your helmet..." Alex tugged at the strap, but he was gone.

"Stupid law anyway," he shouted back to her. "It's more fun without it!"

Alex watched as Adam set up for a jump. He had on a grey hoodie with an anime skateboarder on the back, baggy jeans, and blue sneakers—skate shoes, he called them.

He was flying towards her. He let out a loud whoop and leapt off the board into the air...

Alex opened her eyes, a tear trickling onto her cheek. The familiar dream was fading along with the achingly real sound of Adam's whoop of excitement. Alex lay there, wishing she could turn back time and fix everything, like they did in science fiction movies. Fix Adam, fix her parents...fix herself.

Sunlight was streaming through the window and a rumbling sound filled the air. She lay still, cocooned in her comforter in the cool early morning. Turning her head, she discovered the source of the mysterious noise. Two bright green eyes surrounded by orange fur were six inches from her face.

"Morning, Marty," she sniffed, reaching over to pat the chubby tabby snuggled by her side. The engine sound got louder as Marty purred and closed his eyes, his long tail swishing back and forth.

If only a pat on the head was all that people needed too, Alex thought, rubbing her eyes with her other hand. Cats were cool. She had wanted one ever since she could remember. When she and Adam were ten, her parents had said they could get a pet. But they'd argued so much about whether to get a dog or a cat that they had ended up with neither.

Alex reached under her pillow, pulling out her brother's picture. She stared at Adam's smiling face. He had been so mad at her. He didn't care that she was terrified of dogs. He didn't care about the reason, either—that Spike had attacked her in first grade.

She shivered, her arms exploding instantly in tiny goosebumps. Spike was the gigantic German shepherd her neighbours kept chained in their yard. Alex never knew why, but he would run towards her every time she walked by, almost choking on his chain as he jumped and snarled. He didn't do it to anyone else. One particular day, he broke free and chased her down the street. She tripped and he jumped on her back, ripping her new blue coat and biting her ear.

Adam blamed her when they took Spike away, saying that he only barked at her because she was a chicken and that Spike had sensed her fear and was just being a dog. "You're afraid of everything," he'd said. That's when he'd started calling her a wuss.

Alex used to think he was being mean when he teased her. Now, it was just one more thing she felt guilty about. "Sorry you never got your puppy dog," she whispered.

Carefully, she lifted the tabby out of her way and slid off the bed, then put him back. Marty immediately curled up on the vacated pillow, snuggling into the depression Alex's head had made.

"You're lucky to be a cat. Being a person is way too hard." Marty blinked his already half-closed eyes at her and flipped the tip of his tail. A second later, he was asleep.

Alex tugged the window all the way open and stuck her head out. Dew glistened on the grass and a wispy mist hung low to the ground. Aunt Sophie's chickens were already making the rounds. Four fluffy yellow chicks were clucking below her window, following in a straight line behind their mom.

The smell of fresh coffee drifted down the hall. Aunt Sophie must be up. Alex changed into shorts and a T-shirt. As she brushed her teeth, she pulled back the bandage on her forehead to inspect her wound. Near her hairline, there was an angry red gash with zigzag stitches surrounded by a wicked dark purple bruise—ick! But at least she didn't have a headache this morning, and the goose egg was gone.

She peeled the old bandage with its smear of dried blood the rest of the way off and tossed it in the garbage. Rooting through the pile of supplies from the hospital, she gingerly cleaned her cut, and put on a fresh, smaller bandage. So close to her hairline, it was now barely visible.

Aunt Sophie was alone in the kitchen watering her plants. She was wearing cut-off jean shorts and a wild multicoloured tank top, with her long blonde hair pulled back in a loose braid. There was a tiny tattoo of a star on her back peeking out above the rim of her top. A copper, hand-painted watering can sat at her feet.

Alex could hear her whispering as she plucked dead blooms from the African violets perched on the windowsill.

"Are you talking to the plants?"

Aunt Sophie jumped, bumping the can. Water splashed over the rim. "Good grief, don't scare me like that! I thought you were still in bed."

"Where is everyone?"

"Your mom's still sleeping. And your dad must have stayed in Digby last night."

"That's weird. Mom's always up before me." She gazed out the window. Why hadn't her dad come? Guess she couldn't blame him, really. He probably didn't like the constant fighting either.

"I don't think she slept much last night."

"Oh." Alex knew what that was like. She scanned the table. "Are those Eva's ham and cheese rolls?"

"Yup, she dropped off a pile of baking yesterday before we came home. She's such a doll. Addicted already, huh?"

Alex pursed her lips but didn't answer. "Can I try some?" she asked, pointing to the coffeepot.

"Sure, a small one. But you probably won't like it." Aunt Sophie dumped a handful of the dead blooms into the organic waste. "It's a bit of an acquired taste."

Alex pulled a mug from the cupboard and halffilled it with coffee. She topped it up with cream and two heaping teaspoons of sugar. With hardly a pause, she took a big drink.

"Aha, not your first cup of java, I see."

Alex shrugged sheepishly. "There's a coffee shop across from school."

"Something your mother doesn't know, I'm sure," Aunt Sophie said as she plucked more dead blooms.

"What don't I know?"

Her mother stood at the foot of the stairs. She was still in her nightgown and her hair looked like a tangled bird's nest. "That had better not be coffee."

"Umm…"

"Nice supervision there, sis!" Her mother poured herself a cup and sat at the table.

"She's not a baby, Colleen. Anyway, I told her she could try a taste."

"A taste? She hangs out at the coffee shop across from her school every day. She's probably drunk more coffee than you have."

Alex sputtered her mouthful back into her mug. "You know about that?"

Her mother raised her eyebrows. "You think I've never seen you run back across the street when I come to pick you up?"

"No."

"Yeah, I know…definition of a mother—deaf, dumb, and blind," she muttered. Then she glanced at the basket of baked goodies in the middle of the table. "Who are you and what have you done with my disaster-in-the-kitchen of a sister?"

"Hey!" Aunt Sophie protested. "I can bake."

"Really? Is this the same sister who started a fire in home ec class that shut the entire school down for a week?"

"Oh, that." She waved a dismissive hand at Alex's mother. "Totally not my fault. Those ovens were from the dark ages. I'm pretty sure they found it was something electrical—a short or whatever."

"Uh-huh."

While her mother was distracted, Alex gulped down

another mouthful, savouring the rich flavour. It was way better than the coffee shop stuff.

"Enjoy it, Alex—that's your one and only."

Rats! Her mother didn't miss much...when she bothered to pay attention. Alex plunked down on a chair and loaded a plate with Eva's delights.

A car door slammed.

Her mother twitched in her chair, as though someone had poked her. Aunt Sophie was clutching a handful of dead flowers, her eyes glued to her sister.

That must be Dad, Alex thought. Where had he been all night?

CHAPTER TWENTY-ONE

HER MOM LEAPT UP AND sprinted towards the stairs, but then paused and seemed to change her mind. She swung around, returned to the table, and picked up her coffee. The mug shook and liquid splashed over the rim onto the table, but she didn't seem to notice.

Footsteps echoed on the back walkway outside. There was a soft rap and then the squeak of the screen door opening. Her dad strode through the doorway into the kitchen and stopped abruptly. "Oh! Everyone's up early."

"Dad! What happened? You were supposed to stay here last night."

Her mom didn't even acknowledge him, just continued staring at the wall and drinking her coffee.

"I tried. But I got tied up in Digby and missed the last ferry. Just got in."

"Nice try, Douglas. The ferry runs twenty-four hours a day." Her mom's voice sliced across the room.

Her dad's smile disappeared and his voice got more serious. "That's not what the guy at the gas station in Digby told me. Anyway, I'm here now." Her father seemed to focus all his attention on Alex. "What did you want to do today, Munch?"

She shrugged, glancing between her dad and her mom. "There's nothing much to do here unless you want to go whale watching."

"So you can fall again? I don't think so." Her mother turned in her chair and pointed at Alex. "You're staying on land, where it's safe."

"It'll be all right," Aunt Sophie chipped in. "I'll keep an eye on her."

"Sure, whatever you want," her dad said. "Today is your day."

"Of course you'd say that, Douglas—anything to disagree with me," her mother said. "Well, I'm coming along to keep an eye on you, Alex."

"Now what, Colleen? Is that your way of telling me I can't take care of my own daughter?"

"Think what you want."

Alex gritted her teeth. "If you're going to fight I only want Aunt Sophie to come."

Her father sighed and ran his hand through his hair. "We're not fighting. Everything's fine."

Her mom glared at her dad, but didn't say anything.

Saying it's fine doesn't make it fine, Alex thought. *Does he think I'm dumb?*

"Mom, if you come, you have to promise to be nice to Gus." Alex thought again of the train wreck she had caused the night before, spilling Gus's secret about his feelings for Eva. Maybe if her mom were nice, Alex wouldn't feel so bad about that.

Her mom's face flushed. "I may have overreacted a bit."

"You really hurt his feelings. Anyway, we better get going so we're not late," Alex said. Seeing Daredevil was the only thing she could think of that would make the day bearable. She went upstairs to get her pack.

Marty was still curled up on her pillow. The sunlight flickering through the curtains made dancing patterns on her bed. A dragonfly hovered for a moment in the window frame. Alex was mesmerized by its green-blue, shimmering body. *That must be where its name comes from. That's what dragon skin would look like*, she thought, before it zoomed out of sight. Alex stood there, reluctant to return to the kitchen and her bickering parents.

"All right there, kiddo?"

Alex whirled around. Aunt Sophie was standing in the doorway.

"Yeah, why?"

"A lot going on around here. Just wondering."

"I'm fine."

Aunt Sophie stared at Alex for a long moment. "I'm here if you want to talk."

Alex didn't answer, lowering her gaze and sifting through her pack until Aunt Sophie left. Her hand closed around something small and cool in the bottom. She pulled it out. Adam's knife. Opening the blade, she ran her finger gently along the edge and then turned it over, fingering the etched initials. ACE—Adam Christopher Elliot.

She pushed her finger harder against the sharp edge and winced as it pierced her skin. *Blood brother, blood sister,* she thought as she sucked the blood from the cut. Wiping the blade clean on the side of her pack, she then tucked the knife into the front pocket of her jeans.

As she was about to leave the room, she noticed the bouquet of flowers sitting on the dresser. Aunt Sophie must have put them there. It was full of those yellow blooms her aunt had said were endangered—mountain something or other. No wonder Aunt Sophie had been ticked.

But it wasn't any use being ticked now—they were cut, dead. She couldn't stand to look at them and yanked them out of the vase, tossing them out the window. The wind caught the flowers as they flew through the air and scattered them across the grass.

The walk down the hill seemed much longer than when she and Aunt Sophie had done it alone. Her mother was walking way ahead of the rest of them and her dad had retreated behind his sunglasses. This was going to be fun. For a moment, Alex wished her parents weren't there.

"So, how were your meetings yesterday, Douglas?" Aunt Sophie asked.

Her dad's head whipped around. "What do you mean by that?"

"Nothing."

"I told you, the guy said the ferry was closed," her dad said through gritted teeth.

"Hey, relax. I'm just trying to make conversation."

"The meetings were fine." Her dad sighed and added

softly, maybe so Alex's mom wouldn't hear, "Look, I just wasn't up for more arguing last night, okay?"

Aunt Sophie bit her lip and nodded stiffly, falling back into silence. It felt like forever before they were in sight of the *Evania Rose*. When they passed the café, Alex peered in, but couldn't see Eva. She might have been in the kitchen cooking, but no tempting smells drifted from the open window. Was everything okay? Maybe she was upset about the night before. *Me and my big mouth!* Alex thought.

Strolling along the wooden wharf, Alex couldn't help but notice how much easier the walk was in her own sneakers. She couldn't say the same for her parents. Her father's muttered curses drifted back to her as he tripped over the popping planks. Her mom stumbled a couple of times too, her heeled sandals wobbling on the uneven surface.

Alex eyed the boat bobbing gently on the waves and felt her stomach flip. But it was only a little flip, not nearly as bad as last time. Maybe she was getting used to it. Or maybe it was because she wasn't even a bit wobbly in her own shoes.

Suddenly a red blur was racing towards her. "I'm so happy you're not dead!" the bundle cried, launching itself at Alex, who was then wrapped in a hug that sucked her breath away.

"Hi, Rachel."

"I'm so, so, so sorry!" she sobbed into Alex's shoulder. "It was all my fault, wasn't it? Can you ever forgive me?"

Alex pulled Rachel's arms from their death grip around her neck. "What are you talking about?"

Round eyes filled with tears blinked at her. "You know, 'cause I was talking too much, like I always do. Mom says, 'Rachel, hold your breath for a second, think about what you want to say, then talk,' but I never do," she sniffed.

"It wasn't that."

"You mean you weren't running away from me?"

"No."

"I thought you were mad, you know, when I said you were poor because you were wearing boys' shoes...hey, you got new sneakers!"

"No, I wasn't mad." Alex bit back the sudden urge to smile. Rachel was so sincere, it was hard to be upset with her.

"Stupendous!" Rachel beamed and wiped her tears away. Grabbing Alex's hand, she tugged her towards the boat. "Come on, then."

Alex let herself get dragged on board, hopping over the sliver of water between the dock and boat with barely a blink. Rachel was blathering non-stop, making Alex feel like she'd been sucked into a swirling, chattering tornado.

CHAPTER TWENTY-TWO

"UNCLE GUS, LOOK WHO I found." Rachel had her arm linked with Alex's.

Gus bent his tall frame to duck through the doorway from the cabin. "Nice to have my two spotters back together," he grinned.

Alex slowly wiggled out from Rachel's grip, pretending to dig into her pack. Gus still didn't seem upset. She had kind of expected him to change his mind, convinced she'd ruined his life by revealing his secret love for Eva. But he was his normal cheery lion self. Somehow, that made her feel worse. She almost wished he would be mad.

"Yes, but no ladders this time, Alex," her mom said. She stepped precariously onto the boat, teetering slightly on her heels. Her dad reached out his hand to help her, but she didn't take it. Instead, she grabbed the side of the boat.

Her father dropped his arm and turned away.

Alex sighed, remembering how Gus had been looking at Eva the night before.

As her mom straightened up, she seemed to notice everyone watching her. She glanced at Alex's father's back, then proceeded over to where Gus stood. "I want to apologize for my outburst yesterday," she said, holding out her hand. "I understand it was an accident. I didn't mean to imply otherwise."

Gus's face split into a huge grin as he took her outstretched hand. "Accepted, ma'am. Don't blame you for being upset—any parent would be."

"It's been...difficult lately." Her mom's voice cracked and she looked over at Alex's father again.

"Uh..." Gus seemed at a loss for something to say.

"Looks like a good day for spotting," Aunt Sophie chimed in. She gave her sister's shoulder a quick squeeze and plunked her bags on the bench. "Are we waiting for anyone else?"

"Nope, I had my buddy's son take the tourist crowd this morning on his whale watch. He's just startin' out and appreciates the business. Thought you'd like a private ride."

"Great!" Alex said. "Who needs another whiner like that golf guy, right, Gus?"

"Oh yeah, a real treat, that fella," Gus laughed. "Would you believe, he and his wife sent a thank-you e-mail to our website? Said it was the best time they ever had and they were going to recommend it to all their friends." He scratched his head. "No end of surprises in this business."

They were soon leaving the harbour. Her mom was looking at the reference books in the sheltered cabin area at first. Dad sat beside Alex on the open deck. Then when her mom came out, her dad went in. It was like watching boys and girls picking seats at the school dance, each trying to stay as far away from the other as possible. Inside the cabin, the wheelhouse door was open and Gus was at the helm.

Rachel and Alex pointed out the herons in the trees and talked about the tides as Alex's parents asked questions. Because they weren't sitting together, Alex had to go back and forth to show things to her dad, then repeat everything a second time for her mom. She felt like telling them to look it up, but of course didn't. At least they weren't fighting. Besides, Rachel covered up for Alex's lacklustre answers, acting bubbly enough for ten people.

"How do you know all this, Alex?" her mom asked. "I didn't know you were so interested."

Alex shrugged. "I just remember what I heard from the other tour, I guess." She didn't mention Daredevil, glancing after Rachel, who had gone up to chat with Gus in the wheelhouse.

They motored through the waves, seeing a few solo humpbacks over the next two hours. Sockeye made an appearance—Alex recognized his underbite. He kind of did look like a salmon. But there was no sign of Rooftop and Daredevil. They were nearing the end of the tour as they approached Seal Cove.

"Whale blow ten o'clock!"

At the sound of Gus's voice over the speaker, Alex instantly sprinted to the other side of the boat, searching the horizon with her binoculars for the telltale plume of water and steam.

"There!"

Alex followed the direction of Aunt Sophie's extended arm. "Who is it, Aunt Sophie? Can you tell? Is it Rooftop?"

"Hold your horses, kiddo. I need to get a good look at the flukes. It's right over towards Seal Cove."

"You really like Rooftop, huh?" Rachel asked.

"I guess so," Alex said. "But it's her baby, Daredevil, that I like best."

"Her baby has a name already?" Rachel asked, looking curiously out at the water. "I didn't know that."

"I named him. Well, sort of. Gus called him a daredevil first and then I thought—"

Rachel rolled her eyes. "Please! You can't name him. It's only the science people that do that. You're not a scientist!"

"So? That's what I'm calling him."

"Bogs!" Rachel said, scrunching her nose. "Well… maybe there's something on his flukes, a pitchfork design or horn shapes or something. That would be cool, I guess. Then maybe the scientists would use the name you picked."

"Yeah, maybe."

They steamed across the remaining distance to Seal Cove. Gus cut the engine and joined them on the open deck. As they scanned the waves, the large whale breached the surface. Aunt Sophie and Gus identified it at the same time: "Rooftop!"

"Oh, Daredevil must be close too!" Rachel squealed. "We'll see if there's a design on his flukes."

It would be neat to name him for real, Alex thought. Peering through her binoculars, she waited for the baby to appear.

They drifted in silence. Seal Cove. Alex could hear the seals barking from the shore. Fog had descended down the bank, obliterating the shoreline. A few seals bobbed close to the boat, but scattered as Rooftop breached. In between leaps, she raced back and forth between the boat and Seal Cove, parallel to the shore.

"Wow, she's got lots of energy today," Aunt Sophie said, snapping away with the camera.

Rooftop soared in the air again and again. Alex searched for signs of Daredevil, but Rooftop was alone.

"Where's her baby?" Rachel asked. "Isn't the baby supposed to be right beside her?"

Gus frowned. "Well, the calf would be several months old now, so he can survive for a time on his own," he murmured, rubbing his chin. "That little spitfire has probably wandered off again."

"Where would he go?" Rachel asked.

"Not too far, we hope. He's always found his way back to his mum before."

Alex leaned over the side, like she had done the first time she'd seen him, and stretched her hands out as close to the water as she could. The padding from the life jacket kept the railing from digging too hard into her ribs. But she wobbled as she stretched even farther.

"Be careful!" Her father appeared beside her and put a steadying hand on her back. "What are you doing?"

"Daredevil let me pet him last time. Maybe he'll see me from underwater and come up." Alex squinted, trying to see far down into the depths.

If she had one of those submarines they had on tours in the Bahamas, she could find him. She'd seen it on the DVD her parents had got in the mail last year for their cruise—the cruise they had never gone on.

"What do you mean, you petted him before?" her mother screeched, glaring at Gus.

"Colleen, it's all right," her dad said. "I've got her."

Everyone stared over the side. The minutes ticked by. Even the seals quieted down. The only one still going crazy was Rooftop. The waves got bigger each time she crashed back down from a breach. It made it almost impossible to see under the water.

"Well," Gus said finally, "can't hang around here anymore. We've got to head back in." He returned to the controls and the engine roared to life.

"C'mon Alex," her dad said, tugging her backward. "It's time to leave."

Alex stared at Rooftop as they steamed away. She was still in the same spot, leaping from the sea.

Did Rooftop know something was wrong? Is that what whales did when they were upset? Maybe it was their way of screaming to the world. Only the world wasn't listening.

Alex felt the tension building up inside her.

Where was Daredevil?

CHAPTER TWENTY-THREE

STARING AT THE SPOT WHERE Rooftop had been long after she had disappeared into a tiny speck, Alex wondered where the baby whale could be. Was he hurt? Was he lost?

What if Daredevil never came back?

"What's the matter?" Rachel said. "You look weird."

"Nothing," Alex muttered.

"You keep looking where that whale was," she said. "Are you sad about the baby?"

"He'll be okay."

"Not likely," Rachel said sadly. "I read about it before."

"What did you read?"

"That the babies can't live without their mothers." She pointed to the table with the reference books. "They need milk. If he's not with her, he's probably…" Rachel's voice trailed off.

"What?"

"Dead."

"No," Alex choked. Images flooded her head. The hospital, Adam's pale white face, the closed eyes Alex would have given anything to see open again.

"Sorry."

"He's fine. He has to be."

"Sorry." Rachel's face crumpled.

Alex's hands trembled and her legs started to shake. "Adam can't be dead."

"What did you say?" her mother asked from her seat on the opposite side of the deck.

"Nothing." Alex curled up on the bench, shivering, and gazed out to sea. It was Adam's face, rather than the image of Daredevil, that hovered in front of her blurred vision like a ghost.

Rachel sat down and clasped Alex's hand. Her heat felt good on Alex's icy skin—the one warm spot on her shivering frame. Neither one of them said a word all the way back to port.

At Eva's, Alex sat at the table with everyone else. Eva put a glass of milk in front of her—she drank it. Rachel buttered a scone and passed it to her—she ate it. She said please and thank you in the right places.

But it felt strange—as if she was there, but at the same time she wasn't.

No one seemed to notice but Rachel. It was kind of funny, since Rachel knew her the least of anyone. Gus was making googly eyes at Eva. Eva was batting her eyelashes at Gus and giggling like a girl. Her parents were concentrating so much on ignoring each other that Alex was sure the building could have fallen down around them and they wouldn't have noticed.

So, that left Alex...and Rachel. After they'd eaten, Rachel grabbed her by the hand and tugged her down the aisle to the back of the store, away from the adults.

"My parents are divorced too," Rachel whispered in her ear. "It's not so bad."

"What?" Alex was startled. "My parents aren't divorced."

"They're not?"

"No!"

"Really?" Rachel looked puzzled. "They act just like my parents."

"They do?" Divorced? The word echoed inside of her head. Well, wasn't this what she'd been scared of ever since they'd started arguing all the time? It wasn't really a surprise, was it?

"My parents aren't very nice to each other either," Rachel murmured. "They fight all the time and they stopped holding hands and kissing a long time before they got divorced."

That was exactly how Alex's parents were, at least since Adam's accident. Before that, they used to hug and laugh all the time. It was her fault, she knew. Her fault that Adam was dead, and her fault that her parents hated each other. And now divorce! She'd have no family at all.

Rachel lagged behind with Alex as they all headed back up the hill to Aunt Sophie's after lunch. Her mom and Aunt Sophie walked far in front. Her dad was walking behind the two sisters, talking on his cell phone again. Rachel and Alex walked even slower, getting farther and farther behind.

"Why did your parents get divorced?" Alex asked.

Rachel shrugged. "I don't know."

"There was no reason?"

"Mom always yelled at Dad that he worked too much."

"Oh."

"After they got divorced, Dad married his secretary, Renée."

Alex sighed with relief. Her dad didn't have a secretary.

"Let's go to the lighthouse," Rachel said, pulling Alex by the hand. They passed Aunt Sophie's and continued on the dirt road for several minutes. "It'll take your mind off things—it's really cool."

"I've seen lighthouses before."

"Yeah, but this one's different."

As they rounded another curve in the dirt road, the lighthouse appeared. They walked through the wildflowers and were suddenly surrounded by small rock piles.

"Where did these come from?" Alex asked, amazed. Each one was an inukshuk. She recognized the shape. Her mom had a sculpture of one.

"Tourists make them" Rachel said. "It's the basalt rocks. See how they're broken in kind of rectangles? They make great building pieces—they don't fall over!"

"How do you know about basalt?" The rocky shoreline looked like it had been made of rectangular columns with tall, narrow bricks loosely fitted together.

"I read about it in a book about the island that Gus sent me for Christmas."

"Really?"

"Do you want to make one? An inukshuk, I mean?"

Rachel picked up a loose piece of the basalt rock and offered it to Alex.

"Inukshuk means something like 'we were here,' doesn't it?" Alex said. She remembered that part from an old ad on television.

"I think so."

That was kind of neat—leaving a sign that they had been there. "Okay," she said. Alex picked up more of the loose basalt.

They followed the pattern of the many other inuksuit scattered around them. Alex watched Rachel first before she tried making her own. Alex placed two rocks vertically to form the base for her inukshuk and thought about Adam. Then she placed two long pieces sideways on top of the base, ones for her mom and dad, and a smaller one on top for herself.

She stood back and surveyed her finished work. Maybe this could be some kind of sign—something to show that her family wasn't falling apart after all.

"Ours are the best!" Rachel danced in a circle around their creations. "Don't you think so?"

"Yeah, they're kind of neat, I guess," Alex said. She dug through her bag and pulled out Aunt Sophie's extra camera. Rachel posed by hers and Alex took a picture. Then she took a few of her own inukshuk. She looked at it on the screen—a sculpture of her family.

Rachel chattered all the way back to Aunt Sophie's. They cut across the lawn, passing under Alex's bedroom window.

Rachel stopped suddenly. "What are those?"

"Huh?"

"They look like the flowers I picked for you." Rachel held up a handful of the Eastern Mountain Avens.

"Um…" Alex stared at the blooms. What could she say?

"You threw them away?" Rachel said in a hurt voice. "It took me all afternoon to find them."

"Sorry…I have this thing about dead flowers."

"But they're still green, and the petals—"

"Once you pick them, they're dead."

"Oh," Rachel said in a small voice.

Alex looked at Rachel's sad face. She was about to say something when she heard angry voices coming from inside. Her parents were fighting again.

CHAPTER TWENTY-FOUR

ALEX AND RACHEL TIPTOED THROUGH the hallway from the back door. The voices got louder as they got closer to the kitchen.

"Colleen, I can't figure out what you want!"

"What I want?"

Alex was peering around the doorframe with Rachel pressed against her back. Aunt Sophie was nowhere to be seen. Her dad was sitting at the kitchen table and her mom was leaning against the counter

"You wanted me out...so I left. You can't seem to stand the sight of me, and now you think I'm seeing someone else?" Her dad pinched the bridge of his nose with his fingers.

"Where were you last night?"

"We've been through this already. I thought I'd missed the last ferry."

"So you said."

"Enough of this, Colleen! No more games."

"What's that supposed to mean?"

"Let's be honest and get to what this is really about." Her dad stood up and paced back and forth. "I miss him too."

"This is not about Adam!"

"Of course it is!" Her dad stopped in front of her mom. "You just won't admit it. How are we going to get past this if we never talk about it?"

"Douglas—"

"I see it in your eyes every time you look at me," he declared. "You blame me."

"That's not true."

"You didn't want him to have that skateboard. But he wanted it so badly I bought it anyway. He'd been asking for one for years. I remember, at his birthday party, you said he was too reckless and almost refused to let him keep it."

"He thought he was invincible." Her mom's voice was shaking.

"You see, I knew it!" he said.

"You wouldn't listen to me..." she trailed off, staring out the window. "He was so fearless. My little daredevil—I shouldn't have let him have it."

"I guess it doesn't matter now, does it? It's too late." Her dad took his keys out of his pocket. "Look, I rented a place in the city. I'll get the rest of my stuff out when I get back."

"You're moving out?" Alex raced into the room and grabbed her dad's sleeve.

"Alex, where did you come from?" her mom gasped.

"I'm so sorry, Munch." Her dad gripped her shoulders and stared intently into her eyes. "We didn't want you to find out this way."

Alex pressed her face into his shirt. "You're leaving 'cause of me, aren't you?" she mumbled.

"Of course not," he said, stroking her hair. "We love you very much."

"Is it because Mom isn't nice to you anymore?" Alex cried. "Say you're sorry, Mom."

"Munch…" her dad sighed.

Alex stared up at him with teary eyes. "Don't leave. If you love me, you won't leave."

"It's not that simple," her mom whispered.

"Yes it is!"

"Your dad and I just can't be together right now. We're arguing all the time. That's not a good environment for you or for us."

"Are you getting a divorce?" Alex hiccuped.

Her parents looked at each other. Neither one said anything.

"We're broken, but we're still a family. If you leave, we won't even be a broken one."

"I'll still see you all the time," her dad said.

"I heard you talking about Adam," Alex said to her mom. "It wasn't Dad's fault. He wasn't even there. It was me. I did it. And now you're getting divorced because of it." Tears streamed down her face. "So this is my fault too."

"No, sweetheart, that's not true." Her mom tried to hug her. "None of this is your fault."

Alex pulled away. "It is. You know it is!" she cried. She turned and ran from the kitchen.

"Alex, wait…" her mom called.

"Let her go, she's upset."

Her parents' words followed her as the screen door slammed behind her. Alex raced blindly up the hill. She had to get away. She wasn't even paying attention to where she was going.

"Alex, wait up!" Rachel cried.

She ran and ran. Then the lighthouse was looming in front of her. Alex ran towards the cliff, not watching where she was going. She veered off the path. Thick bundles of purple thistle scratched her arms and legs.

Alex struggled through the brush, focused on her goal. She rushed up to the inukshuk she had created just a short while ago. Rage and frustration surged up within her as she stared at it. It wasn't a symbol of her family, it wasn't anything at all.

With a loud cry, she kicked it. The inukshuk collapsed, the rocks scattering wide. Grabbing them one by one, Alex heaved them over the cliff and into the sea. "Why did you have to die?" she screamed. Sobbing, she fell to her knees.

Arms wrapped around her. "Everything's going to be okay," Rachel murmured.

"It's not fair," Alex moaned.

"No, it's not."

"I miss him so much."

Alex cried into Rachel's shoulder. Rachel stayed by her side until Alex's tears finally stopped. She must have really run out of them this time. They sat quietly afterward and watched the waves.

"I don't want to go back yet," Alex said.

"We don't have to. We can go for a walk the opposite way, if you want. Look, there's a path over there."

"All right." She was so glad not to be alone right then.

Alex slowly got to her feet. She realized she still had her pack over her shoulder. Switching it to the other side, she followed Rachel along a beaten-down path through the tall grass. The narrow trail hugged the shoreline.

They walked farther and farther away from the lighthouse, winding inland for a bit before curving back out along the cliffs.

Alex gazed out over the ocean and was surprised to see the horizon had vanished.

The fog had returned.

CHAPTER TWENTY-FIVE

THEY WALKED FOR AGES WITHOUT talking. Rachel reached down as if to pick a flower. Then she stopped and looked back at Alex with a wide smile. "Don't kill the flowers, right?"

"Right."

Rachel brushed her fingertips over the petals of the flower before straightening up and continuing along the trail.

"What was he like?"

"Who?"

"Your brother. I don't have any brothers or sisters. What was he like?"

Alex walked for a while and thought about Adam. "He was totally different from me," she finally said.

"I thought you were twins." Rachel turned around with a puzzled expression.

"Oh, we looked alike." Alex pulled the folded photo from her pocket and showed it to Rachel. They were side by side, with the same dark, wavy hair and grey eyes.

"He's cute."

"That was right before he took Dad's electric razor and shaved his head."

Rachel's laugh tinkled through the air. "Bald?"

"As a bowling ball." Alex smiled at the memory. "He said the older boys at the skate park all shaved their heads and that it was cool. Mom didn't think so."

"Did he get in trouble?"

Alex shook her head. "Nope. But he had to let it grow out to a buzz cut."

"He sounds like fun."

"Mm-hmm," Alex nodded. "I remember when I was little and I got my first two-wheel bike. It was dark green and I hated the colour. I wanted purple but they didn't have any. When I went out the next day to ride it, my whole bike was painted purple. Adam snuck into Mom's sewing room and stole her craft paint."

"Cool."

"Every bit was covered in different shades of purple—the spokes, the handle bars, the seat…and the floor of the garage." Alex laughed and swallowed the sudden lump in her throat. "The girls on my street thought it was ugly."

"Bogs!" Rachel huffed. "It sounds perfect."

"It was—I loved it. Even when the paint started peeling off." Alex sighed. "I had forgotten all about that." *Another perfect memory,* she thought.

They stopped and watched a monarch butterfly flutter around them in a circle. It landed on a tall flower, its wings barely moving.

"Did you do lots of stuff together?" Rachel asked wistfully.

"Sometimes," Alex said.

"Like what?"

"We used to go exploring behind our house—it was a greenbelt. Adam is...was...a great tree climber."

"I love to climb trees too," Rachel said, looking around. "Should we try to find one?"

Alex shook her head.

Rachel looked disappointed as they resumed walking. The landscape was changing. There were fewer trees and the bushes were shorter, more scraggly. Different kinds of plants were lining the path, which had been slowly veering away from the shore. They were now far away from the ocean. Alex could no longer hear the waves.

"Do you live with your mom or your dad?" Alex asked.

"Both."

"How do you do that?"

"I spend two weeks at Dad's and two weeks at Mom's."

"Do you go to the same school?" Dad said he was downtown. Did that mean she'd have to go to two different schools now? Maybe he didn't want her with him at all.

"Uh-huh," Rachel nodded.

"So...do you like one place better than the other?"

Rachel thought for a minute. "Well, Mom and I live in the same house where I always lived. So, I like my room better and everything. But Renée is nice too, and she and Dad made me a cool room."

"So it's good, then?"

"It's okay, I guess." Rachel twirled a twig she'd picked up off the path. "But Mom doesn't like me to talk about how nice Renée is and she always wants to know weird stuff."

"Like what?"

"What kind of furniture they have, what jewellery Renée has, what kind of trips they take, stuff like that."

Alex shrugged. That was weird.

"Will they ever get back together?"

Rachel sighed and shook her head. "I don't think so. Renée is going to have a baby—a girl."

"So you'll have a sister?"

"Yeah, but she'll only be small. It's not like I'll be able to do anything with her. I'll be way too old by the time she can climb a tree."

"Oh, right."

Long, grassy stalks brushed their legs, the path narrower as they strolled slowly along.

"They're moving my room so they can have the nursery next to theirs." The twig snapped in Rachel's hands.

"Oh."

"Forget what I said before." Rachel tossed the twigs into the tall grass. "Divorce stinks."

What if Alex's dad got married again and had another baby? Or her mom got a boyfriend she didn't like? Or they moved away? Nausea swirled inside her.

They walked for a bit longer and came to a big, flat boulder. Rachel and Alex sat cross-legged and shared sips from Alex's bottle of water.

The fog had edged closer, like it was following them.

"Can I ask you something?" Rachel asked.

Alex glanced at her. "Haven't you been already?"

"It's kind of serious."

"I don't know...I guess."

"It's about your brother's accident." Rachel leaned forward.

Alex bit her lip. The skate park flashed in front of her eyes...*Watch this, sis...*

"Sorry, you don't have to."

"I can't." With Adam and now her parents, her whole world had turned into a nightmare. It was hard to talk about. It made it more real somehow.

"Never mind." Rachel jumped up and grabbed Alex's hand. "C'mon."

Rachel dragged her through the grass into the middle of the sea of wildflowers until they found a patch that was flat and open. "Close your eyes."

"No way." Alex thought Rachel had gone totally nutty.

Rachel snorted and placed her hands on her hips. "Close your eyes."

"Fine."

"What do you hear?"

"You, talking like always."

"Stop kidding!" Rachel poked her in the arm. "Concentrate—what do you hear?"

"Nothing? I don't know...the wind through the grass, I guess."

"What else?"

Alex focused on the sounds around her. "I hear bees, a bird chirping, and...no, wait, different kinds of birds... and peepers—I hear peeper frogs."

"Cool, huh?"

"Yeah."

"Now keep your eyes closed."

Alex felt Rachel's hands grab hers and pull. Alex didn't resist, and spun around with her. Soon, they were whirling in circles.

"I have my eyes closed too," Rachel squealed. "It's fun, huh?"

Alex felt lightheaded and floaty. It was kind of silly— like being a little kid again.

Laughing, they both stopped at the same time, wobbling from side to side. "Ooooh, I feel dizzy," Alex said.

"Me too."

Alex opened her eyes and gasped. She couldn't see anything. They had been totally engulfed in white, just like on the whale watch. The fog had snuck up and captured them.

CHAPTER TWENTY-SIX

"UH-OH!" ALEX SAID.

"What's wrong?" Rachel still had her eyes closed and was giggling as she staggered around in a circle.

"Open your eyes."

"It's not as much fun if you do that." Rachel plunked down on the grass.

"We've got a problem."

"You have to go to the bathroom? Just go. I won't watch."

"It's not that!"

"So, what else—oh!" Rachel opened her eyes and gasped.

Alex sat down. The icy fingers of fog brushed against her skin, making her shiver. She rubbed her goosebump-covered arms.

"I can't see anything," Rachel whispered.

"Me neither."

It was pretty creepy. Barely a few feet in any direction were visible. What else was hidden out there, just out of sight?

"How are we going to get home, Alex?"

"Jeez, you're asking *me*? You're the one that's been here before. You tell me!"

Rachel gaped at Alex, her eyes huge. "Yeah, for a few weeks last summer. But I was mostly on the boat with Gus or around his house. He lives on the other side of the island. Over here, I've only been as far as the lighthouse." She looked wildly around her. "And there was no fog! It's like trying to find your way in the dark! I'm scared of the dark. I have a nightlight!"

"Okay, okay, take it easy. Remember on the whale watch before? The fog moves around a lot. It'll probably be gone in a few minutes."

"You think so?" Rachel's voice sounded relieved.

"Sure," Alex said.

They stared at the thick white wall. Every few minutes, Alex would be convinced it had moved—something within the fog would shift. But it must have been her eyes playing tricks on her. Nothing more became visible beyond their same small circle.

Rachel was sighing more loudly by the minute. "Alex…it's not moving!"

"Be patient. It will."

"When? I'm f-freezing!" Rachel griped through chattering teeth.

Alex pulled her bag off her shoulder and looked inside. "Here, take my jacket."

"Don't you want it?"

"We can take turns. You go first."

Rachel quickly thrust her arms into the jacket and wrapped it tightly around her. "Oh, thanks," she sighed. "This feels better."

Trying to take her mind away from her own freezing limbs, Alex dug through the rest of her pack. She found one of Eva's scones wrapped in a paper bag from the other day. It was squished flat, but it would still taste good. It might come in handy later. Stuffed at the bottom was the book on Brier Island plus the map that her aunt had given her.

They smoothed the map out and looked at the various trails. "Which one were we on?" Alex asked, tracing her finger along the shore. "The dotted lines here are marked as hiking trails."

"Your Aunt Sophie's is by the lodge, and that's here," Rachel pointed.

"Right, so we were at the northern lighthouse, then… up here?"

Rachel stared into the fog. "Yeah, and then we walked along the ocean trail for a bit. But then we came into the meadow, remember?"

"So which trail are we on now?" Alex studied the several dotted trails that zigzagged across the map of the island.

"I don't know," Rachel said. "Maybe this one…it comes away from the shore, see? That's what we did."

"We'll just have to find that same trail, that's all."

"But we were spinning in circles with our eyes closed…"

Alex could hear the thud of her heart pounding in the stillness. "So…we don't know which direction will take us back to the ocean, do we?"

"Does it matter? I mean, we can't stay here...what if the fog never leaves?"

Alex didn't know what to do. What if they went farther towards the centre of the island? They could get even more lost. Anxiety rippled through her. She tried to calm her breathing and listen, like they had done before when they played the game. She tried, but she couldn't hear the ocean, just the peepers and birds.

"What are we going to do?"

"Why are you asking me? I don't know!" Alex snapped.

"Sorry," Rachel said. "I thought you'd know what to do. You know, since you used to explore with your brother."

"Adam was the explorer, not me," Alex said, softening her voice. "He always decided where to go. I just followed." She wished he were there now. He'd take charge and blaze on through the fog or whatever else was in their way.

"Oh."

Alex sighed. What were they going to do?

"Alex?"

"Yeah?"

"I was thinking..." Rachel tilted her head and stared into the white.

"About what?"

"Do you think it's like this in heaven? You know, all misty, like living inside a cloud?"

Heaven? The strange feeling returned that there was something hovering out there, just beyond her reach. She wished it was heaven—then she could see Adam.

It would be amazing to be with him again, to hear his laugh. She wouldn't even mind if he teased her.

"Or maybe it's more like sitting on top of the puffy clouds with the sun shining down…you know, like that cream cheese commercial."

Cream cheese? Alex blinked, the spell broken. "Maybe we should just start walking."

"Okay." Rachel stood up. She lifted her foot to take a step, but then stopped.

"What's wrong?"

"Which way?"

"Um." How was she supposed to know? Alex examined the flattened grass around them. One little part by her feet looked a bit more trampled—maybe. "I guess this could be a trail."

"Ooh, I think you're right. You're awesome!" Rachel grabbed her hand. "You lead."

Sucked back into the swirling wind that was Rachel, Alex tentatively led the way through the wall of white.

It seemed to be a path, for a while. Long grass leaned across the narrow clearing as they slowly made their way over the terrain. But the fog was not cooperating at all. It seemed to be getting thicker, if anything.

Alex kept listening, hoping for the sound of ocean waves, but couldn't hear anything above the constant thump of her heart banging against her ribs. Rachel's comment about heaven kept popping back into her head. Maybe he was with her. The swirling white brushed past her like a ghostly whisper.

They'd been walking for ages, and the ground began to feel different under Alex's feet. It was soft and spongy. Did that mean they were close to the ocean? It couldn't. That path had been hard and dry.

"Ew, yuck," Rachel said. "The ground is all squishy!"

"That's odd, it wasn't wet before," Alex said. She looked down, feeling water seep into her sneakers.

"It's covering my shoes!" Rachel cried.

"Stop!"

Rachel froze. The fog chose that moment to drift away from them, widening their circle of vision. Nothing looked familiar. Even the grasses and plants looked a bit different. She was sure they hadn't been this way before.

Alex turned back the way they had come. What she had thought was a path before definitely didn't look like one now. She stared down at her map, her eyes drifting away from the coastline to the centre of the island. If they hadn't found the coastline by now, they must have been going in the wrong direction.

Alex squinted at the markings in the middle of the island map. They looked like sprigs of grass. She compared them to her aunt's hand-drawn legend along the side. It was the symbol for a bog. A bog? Bogs were full of water, weren't they? Water—which was now brimming over the tops of her toes. She was sinking.

Rachel yelped.

Alex looked up from the map. Rachel was already up to her ankles in water. Frantically, Alex scanned their surroundings. There was a small bare patch of ground that wasn't covered in the spongy material they were sinking into.

"Grab my hand," she said. Tugging Rachel sideways, she jumped towards the bare ground. Then she stumbled as Rachel yanked her back.

"What?" she cried.

Rachel whimpered. "I'm stuck."

Alex reached for Rachel's other hand. "Can you pull one of your legs free?"

"Get me out!"

"Stop squirming around—you're making it worse." Alex watched in horror as Rachel sank up to her calves.

"I'm going to get sucked under!" she screamed.

"RACHEL!" Alex bellowed.

Rachel froze, staring at her with frightened eyes.

"I'll get you out, just calm down. Okay?"

Rachel nodded.

"Can you pull one of your legs out?"

"I don't think so."

"Try, okay? And I'll pull at the same time."

Rachel nodded again.

"Okay—one, two, three, pull!" Alex yanked on Rachel's arms as hard as she could. There was a loud squelching noise and Rachel toppled forward. Alex quickly dragged her to the small patch of earth.

Rachel threw her arms around Alex's neck. "You saved my life!"

"Hold on!" Alex said. She got back up and tested the surrounding ground with her feet. It seemed solid enough. And it was dry. "Okay, I think we're safe for now. What is that spongy stuff?"

"I think it's the stuff that grows in bogs. It's got some bizarre name." Rachel said, picking leaves and grass from her bare, wet legs. "Just our luck, getting stuck in a bog! At least my shoes stayed on!"

"Those strange flowers are growing out of it too." Alex pointed to stalks of tall, fleshy, purple and green plants. "They're everywhere."

"When I came here before, I was only on the paths on the other side of the island, but I think that a few of the bogs are bigger, part of some nature reserve."

"Maybe it's in Aunt Sophie's book. That might help us find out where we are exactly." Alex sat cross-legged on the ground and pulled out the plant book. Flipping quickly through the pages, she stopped at a photo of the flowers. "Here—those purple fleshy things are called pitcher plants."

"Oh, I didn't know what they were called."

"And it says they live in bogs in that green spongy goop. It's called sphagnum moss. And it only grows in bogs too. Rats! I was hoping it was just a little patch of something."

"Is this one of the big bogs?" Rachel asked, looking around her with dismay.

"I don't know. There is one that looks sort of big on the map. And there are no paths through it."

"We'll drown!"

"It's not like a lake or anything. It can't be that deep."

Alex looked at the pools of water surrounding them. How deep *was* the water? The book didn't say. She looked back at the map. She hoped they weren't around Big Pond— it looked like a big stretch of water on the map, so it would likely be deep. But that was on the other side of the island. They couldn't have walked that far. Her heart flipped again. "Anyway, you can swim, right?"

"What good is that going to do if we get sucked into that mossy stuff? It'll be like quicksand!"

The moss was everywhere. Alex got one long look at it before the fog dropped back down over them like a curtain. "I guess we're not going anywhere," she whispered.

CHAPTER TWENTY-SEVEN

HUDDLED TOGETHER ON THE TINY bump of dry land, Alex and Rachel shivered with the cold. Waiting for the fog to lift didn't seem like such a good idea after all.

"We have to try to find our way back."

"How?" Rachel asked. "We don't know which way to go."

"Maybe we do. I think that's the direction we came from," Alex said, pointing towards the pale outline of two pitcher plants through the foggy haze. "See where there's one tall one and a shorter one?"

"Not really."

"That's it, I'm pretty sure."

"But it's dry here. What if we both get stuck this time?" Rachel shuddered.

"We won't." Alex stood up and held out her hand. "It'll be easy." It was a odd sensation. Those were almost the same words Adam had said to her a gazillion times.

Rachel pulled her hand from inside the sleeve of Alex's jacket and let Alex tug her to her feet.

Step by step, Alex led them through the bog. The fog had lifted a smidge, so their world got a little bigger. She could see farther ahead than before and got good at spotting plants that didn't grow in the moss. They hopscotched from patch to patch, with Alex in the lead, for what seemed like hours. It kept them out of the water—most of the time.

"Bogs!" Alex hollered as she got another soaker.

"You okay?"

"Fine," Alex muttered. She waved Rachel towards the dry part rather than the wet pool Alex had landed in.

"Bogs?" Rachel said. "You sound like Gus. He says that instead of a curse word." She snorted. "Ha, ha, get it? You said 'Bogs'…and we're in a bog!"

"Very funny." Being the leader wasn't all it was cracked up to be. Alex thought of all the times Adam had guided her over streams, around rocky ground, up into trees. *What would he think now*, she wondered, watching her in the lead? She glanced into the pea soup fog. *Are you there, Adam, watching over me?*

They stood for a few seconds while Alex scanned the plants to decide where they would go next. What was Rachel yipping about now? She sounded like a puppy dog. "What, Rachel?" she grumbled.

"I didn't say anything."

"Yes you did." Alex heard the yipping again. But then she realized it might not be coming from behind her. It was so hard to tell in the thick fog.

"I hear it too. What is it?"

"I don't know, but I think it's coming from over there," Alex said, pointing in front of them. And, was that…the ocean too?

"Kind of sounds like dogs barking, doesn't it? Maybe someone's walking their dogs."

"Barking!" Alex shouted. "It's barking seals. We must be close to Seal Cove. Come on!"

"Wait!"

Alex yanked Rachel towards her. They both splashed through the chilly, ankle-deep water.

"Yuck!"

"Keep going," Alex cried, pulling Rachel along.

"Not so fast!"

"Sorry." Suddenly, they weren't splashing in water anymore. Alex stopped and let go of Rachel's hand.

Rachel gingerly tested the ground, patting it with her foot. Then she jumped up and down. "Woohoo! We're back on real land. We made it. I knew we would!" She rushed over to Alex and grabbed her in another death-grip hug.

Alex squirmed away. Rachel was way too huggy for her liking. She'd maxed out on hugs. Squinting, she looked around. The sun was back. It was creepy the way the fog appeared and disappeared so fast. There wasn't a pitcher plant or any mossy goop in front of them. Just dry ground.

Alex and Rachel walked for several more minutes, up a slight hill and through the knee-high grass and flowers. Then, suddenly, they were back on the path, the ocean laid out in front of them like a shimmering blanket.

The fog was almost gone. It had receded back past the entrance to the cove. The waves sparkled in the sunlight, seeming to celebrate their release from gloom as well.

Seals basked on the rocks and bobbed in the water, barking and yelping to each other. It was as if the white cloud they'd been wrapped in had never existed.

"Let's get home!" Rachel's voice was fading. She had already turned onto the path in the direction of the lighthouse.

"Wait a sec," Alex called. There was a large dark form on the beach, half in and half out of the water. And it was a totally different colour than the rest of the rocks. Was it a shipwrecked boat or something?

Then it moved. Or she thought it did.

Water splashed. Alex's pulse zoomed into overdrive. It wasn't just the waves, was it? Could it be alive?

She rushed to the rocks and scanned for a path down to the water. All the times Adam had to find her a way around rocky obstacles flashed in her head. She'd always avoided climbing rocks whenever she could.

"Alex?" Rachel hollered from down the path. "What are you doing? Let's go."

"There's something on the beach."

Rachel jogged back towards her. "Like what?"

"Maybe a dolphin. But it's kind of big..." Alex's eyes were drawn back to the creature. A sinking feeling washed over her. She remembered Rooftop going crazy at the entrance to Seal Cove on their whale watch earlier in the day. "Oh no, it can't be..."

"Can't be what?"

Alex lifted her gaze to the deeper water. Amongst the whitecaps and scattered seals, a larger form cut through the waves. Rooftop was still there—zooming back and forth. Just then she breached high into the air and crashed back down again.

She was sounding the alarm as best she could—that her baby was in trouble. Alex stared back at the form below her. Daredevil was beached.

CHAPTER TWENTY-EIGHT

"WHAT IS THAT?"

Alex was shaking. What was she going to do? She paced back and forth, searching for an easy way down the cliff.

"It looks like a whale. Is it dead?"

"No, it moved. I'm sure it did. I think…I think it's Daredevil. He's beached!"

"Your baby whale?" Rachel cried. "We should go for help."

"You go," Alex said, her eyes still searching for a path. "He could be hurt. I have to get down there. Maybe I can help him."

She finally spotted a small crevice between two large boulders that didn't seem too treacherous. Placing a hand on one of the boulders, she was suddenly dizzy. When she looked below, the rocks wavered in front of her eyes.

Rachel grabbed her arm. "You can't go down there!"

Alex shrugged her off. "I have to. He's been there for ages already. Rooftop was out there on our whale watch. That was hours ago!" Alex felt sick thinking that Daredevil had been in danger all that time. Her instincts had told her something was wrong with Rooftop's strange behaviour. If only she'd made Gus check it out then.

"Let's go get help," Rachel said.

"That's a good idea. You should hurry."

"What? I'm not leaving you here."

"I'm staying to help Daredevil. Someone has to go down there before it's too late."

"We'll hurry back."

Alex shook her head.

"Well," Rachel frowned. "If that's what you want…"

Then the decision was made for them. Fog wrapped around Alex and Rachel like a fleece blanket, only there was no warmth in it. It was even thicker than before. They stood still, paralyzed. It had happened so fast! Barely time to blink.

They huddled in the chilly air, and then just as quickly it was withdrawing again, a wall hovering just offshore.

Alex glanced down at Daredevil as he thrashed again in the shallow water. He could be running out of time. Whales should be in the water, not on land. "I'm going down there before the fog comes back in."

"I'm not staying up here by myself!" Rachel squealed.

"You're going to get Gus, remember?" Alex turned away, anxious to get down to Daredevil. If she was going to save him, she had to do something, and fast.

"No way!" Rachel pointed to the fog bank. "That could come back any second. Then I'd be lost and alone. Let's go together."

"No! If the fog comes back in, nobody will be able to come back here to help Daredevil." Stepping gingerly on the first boulder, Alex yelped as it shifted under her weight. A few smaller rocks bounced away down the cliff. She pulled back and leaned against the big boulder, closing her eyes. Her bravery had evaporated with a teeny slip of her foot.

Alex sucked in a deep breath. "You can do it," she whispered.

"What did you say?" Rachel asked.

"Nothing." Opening her eyes, Alex saw she was level with patches of burnt-orange and grey lichens clinging to the rock—they looked like crusty mould. Tufts of tall, wheat-coloured grass sprang from the crevices, swaying in the breeze.

Please, make me strong, she prayed. *Please give me a little of Adam's bravery—just a little.* She looked down at Daredevil's lonely silhouette on the beach. His tail flapped lamely. She had to help him. Swallowing hard, she blew out the breath that she'd been holding, and stepped back onto the basalt rocks. Rachel followed closely behind her.

"Go get Gus!"

"He's probably not there anyway. He does a whale watch in the afternoons," Rachel said. "And even if your parents and Sophie are home, they'd have to call the Coast Guard or something, right? How long would that take?"

They both looked at Daredevil. He might not have much time.

"Come on, then," Alex snapped. She figured it was more likely Rachel's fear of the fog that kept her from going for help, but she didn't want to waste another second arguing.

Grabbing at grass where she could, Alex inched her way down the rock wall. Before taking each step, she tested it lightly with one foot first, making sure it was stable.

It was hard. Sharp rocks scraped their arms and legs. Sweat dripped into their eyes as they baked under the hot sun. Alex almost wished the cool fog would return. It had retreated farther out into the cove and sunlight was sparkling on the water.

For the last several minutes, the rocks had been covered in seaweed. This made the going even more hazardous, as their feet and hands slipped on the slick piles. Puddles of warmed seawater rippled in the hollows of flatter rocks. Time seemed to stand still as their world became the next rock, the next foothold. It felt like it would never end. Her heart skipped a beat. Maybe this hadn't been such a good idea.

"Watch this big one beside me," Alex called up. "It's loose."

"Okay," Rachel gasped.

Searching for the next foothold, Alex glanced below her and realized she didn't have to look anymore—they'd finally made it down to the beach. Sagging with relief, she reached up a supporting hand to steady Rachel as she jumped down the last few feet.

Alex gulped as she looked back up at how far they had descended. She didn't even want to think about the journey they'd have to make back up the cliff. But she'd done it. Adam would have been proud of her, she was sure. *Not always a wuss, am I, Adam?*

As they approached Daredevil, the whale seemed to become aware of their presence. He thrashed around, his tail smacking loudly on the shallow water.

"He's scared," Alex said. Instinctively, she slowed her steps and spoke in a low voice. "It's okay, Daredevil. We won't hurt you."

Rachel stayed close behind her.

"We're here to help you," Alex continued.

"Oh, poor guy!" Rachel cried. Her loud voice rang across the silent cove.

Daredevil twisted again, lifting his head off the beach.

"Shh, Rachel, not so loud. You're scaring him!"

"Oops! Sorry."

"It's okay, Daredevil." Alex moved forward to stand beside the whale. He was huge this close up. Alex guessed he had to be almost twenty feet long and taller than Alex's five feet and two inches. Daredevil wasn't anything like a baby. It quickly became obvious why he was beached, though. Several loops of fishing line were tangled around him, attached to two buoys that floated behind him in the water.

White crystals were crusted in his eyes and around his mouth. Sand and small rocks were stuck to his sides and underneath his jaw, caught in his throat grooves. Alex could see long dark marks crisscrossing his grey skin, which was dull and dry.

Tears welled in her eyes as she watched him writhing around. "Shh," she whispered, her voice cracking. "Shh."

The back part of Daredevil's body, past his tangled

long flippers, was in the shallow water. His skin was wet and shiny there, coated from the spray each time he smacked his tail.

"Water! He needs water on the rest of his skin," Alex said. "We'll get him wet and then try and get this line off him."

"How are we going to do that?"

Alex looked frantically around. It wasn't as if buckets were just magically going to appear. What would hold water? "Pass me my jacket."

Rachel looked puzzled as she untied the jacket from around her waist and handed it to Alex. "What are you going to do with that?"

"It's waterproof. We can use it like a scoop."

"You really think that will work?"

It has to, Alex thought. She ran to the water's edge. "Help me," she called out. "Hold the other side."

They pushed the jacket under the water and pulled it back up. Water poured over the sides, but much remained in the middle. The splashing salt water licked painfully at their scratched legs.

They shuffled sideways to Daredevil's head, trying carefully not to slosh too much over the sides.

Gently tipping the water out, they let it cascade over Daredevil's side. As soon as the water touched his skin, Daredevil froze. Alex and Rachel moved the jacket from side to side as the water poured out, covering as much of him as they could. They couldn't reach the very top of his body, but were able to cover most of his side.

Alex was thrilled it had worked. They raced back to the water's edge. Again and again, they scooped up water and splashed it over Daredevil's massive form. They tried to fling it high enough to cover his head, but it was hard to tell if it made it all the way over him.

Alex thought maybe the whale understood they were trying to help him. She hoped so. She kept murmuring reassuring words as they made their way to and from the water. She had no idea how much time had passed. There was only the motion of filling the jacket and pouring the water, filling the jacket and pouring the water.

The sun beat down from a now-cloudless sky. After a while, Alex noticed the splashes from Daredevil's tail were getting smaller and smaller. She looked with frustration out at the fog bank hovering beyond the edges of the cove. "Fog! Come back in and hide the sun!" she cried.

Daredevil's body jerked.

"Sorry." Alex's head was pounding and her arms ached. Her lips were cracked and dry.

"I can't even lift my arms anymore," Rachel said. She dropped the jacket.

Alex ignored her, smoothing water with her hand around Daredevil's face. She rinsed away some of the tiny stones and sand. "There," she soothed, "doesn't that feel better?"

She thought about the damp facecloth she would soak in water to moisten Adam's lips every day. She'd whispered the same things to him.

But it seemed like Daredevil's skin was getting drier, not wetter. The sun dried the water as fast as they poured it.

CHAPTER TWENTY-NINE

"WE NEED SOMETHING TO KEEP him wet. His skin is drying out too fast!"

Rachel came over to stand beside her. "What about if we dunk the jacket again and cover him with that?"

"We can't." Alex shook her head. "We need it to carry the water."

"Oh, right."

Looking around for inspiration, Alex noticed how the thick seaweed was covering everything. Seaweed! When they were climbing down the rocks, it had still been wet, even though the tide was out. It must keep water inside it.

"Rachel, get some seaweed and soak it in the water. Then put it on his back."

Rachel scrunched up her face. "Yuck, seaweed? It's slimy!"

"But it might help him. Then we can try to get the fishing line untangled." Alex grabbed a fistful, dragged it through the salt water, and laid it carefully on Daredevil's skin. Some of it slid to the ground, but most of it stuck.

Reenergized, she grabbed more bunches already in the water and placed them wherever she could on Daredevil. Rachel also began picking up loose seaweed and kelp strands floating in the water and placing them on the baby whale.

"Ew—this stuff is disgusting."

Alex lost track of how much time had passed. Even though they'd covered most of him with seaweed and his skin was now staying wet, Daredevil was barely moving.

"C'mon, Daredevil, don't give up!"

Daredevil twitched slightly.

"We have to get these lines off him," Alex said. The fishing line was a jumbled mess, wrapped around his body and twisted around his flippers. She remembered Gus talking about an entangled right whale he'd rescued, and how whales needed their flippers for balance and to swim.

Alex leaned forward to examine the line. She ran her fingers over it. It was just rope. Maybe she could cut it. She pulled Adam's knife from her pocket and opened the blade.

"Rachel, try and pull out a piece so I can get the blade under it."

She started sawing on a piece of line with the knife and eventually cut through the threads. But it was hard work and her arms were already aching from carrying the water.

It took a long time to get through one piece of the line—a small victory. There were several more loops to be cut.

Desperately, she started on the next piece. "I'll cut through it all," she vowed. "I will."

Without the constant spray of water, Daredevil's skin was getting drier by the second. "Rachel, get some water on him!"

"I'm sorry, Alex. My arms won't work anymore. I think I'm going to throw up."

"I can't do it all by myself!" Alex tugged at the fishing line again. It wouldn't budge. She'd have to cut every bit off. "Why didn't you stay with your mother like you're supposed to?" she cried at Daredevil. "All the other babies do. Why didn't you?"

The baby flicked his tail weakly. Dread overwhelmed her. He was running out of time, Alex could feel it.

"You *are* just like Adam. Daredevil is the perfect name for you, too. He wouldn't wait for his helmet. Why? I almost had the strap off—only another second and he would have had it." Alex was weeping and muttering to herself as she sawed frantically at the line.

She didn't even pause as she cut through another loop. Immediately, she started on the next, then the next. "Neither one of you did what you were supposed to," Alex raved as she tugged at the line. "And look what happened. You should be out there, safe, swimming with your mom. But no! You decided to go off by yourself."

At that moment, Alex stumbled backward. Dazed, she glanced down to see the knife broken in her hands. Time seemed to stop as she watched the blade fall.

She reached down and fished it out of the water. It had snapped off at the base. There was no fixing it. She slipped the broken blade into her pocket and examined the rest of the fishing line. She had managed to cut through many of the pieces. Maybe that was enough to untangle the rest.

Carefully, she pulled the cut pieces over and under the other loops. It was like trying to un-knot her grandmother's yarn. It took forever to weave the pieces in and out. But finally, a large piece came loose in her hands.

Her heart soared. "Yes!" she cried, tossing the piece of line aside and starting on another piece. It was a bit easier to untangle than the first.

"Alex?"

"Stop complaining and come over and help me!" She'd gotten half the line off now. "It's working."

"No, it's not that." Rachel's voice was quivering. "The tide is coming in."

Alex looked at the small waves that were now lapping around her. She hadn't even noticed. Glancing behind her, she was shocked to see that the water had quietly circled around them and now covered all of the shore. It was at least twenty feet to dry land.

Farther out in the cove, Rooftop was circling closer, too. Biggest tides in the world—twenty feet in six hours, Aunt Sophie had said. Alex looked up at the seaweed clinging to the basalt cliffs far above their heads. They were running out of time, too.

"Hang in there, Daredevil," she said, working faster. "You'll be back with your mom soon." She pulled another loop free.

"Alex?"

"What now?"

"I…I'm trapped."

Alex looked over at Rachel. She was perched on a boulder several feet away and below her, farther out in the cove. It was now surrounded by water. "Why didn't you get off before?"

"I don't know, it didn't seem so bad…and then it was."

"It won't be too deep yet. Jump."

"I can't!"

"You have to. I can't leave Daredevil. Jump down!" Alex said. "You can swim, right? What's the problem? Don't be such a wuss—" Alex paused. She couldn't believe she'd said that. It had hurt every time Adam had called her that.

"I can't help it," Rachel cried. "The water is full of floating seaweed. I can't see where to put my feet. What if I fall in a hole or something?"

The rising tide was now at Alex's calves. Buoyed seaweed smacked against her legs, tossed by the angry waves. Alex shivered, uneasiness rippling through her. *How quickly did the tide come in?* She tried to calculate it in her head. Twenty feet in six hours—that would be more than three feet in an hour, over a foot every twenty minutes. She looked down. In twenty minutes, the water would be past her thighs.

They weren't running out of time—they were out of time.

CHAPTER THIRTY

"ALEX!"

She leaned her forehead against Daredevil's side. More time—she had to have more time. "I'm coming," she said.

Quickly, she loosened two more loops. But no matter how hard she pulled, the rest of the line wouldn't move. It was still wrapped tightly around one of Daredevil's flippers.

Alex pulled the broken blade from her pocket and ran her finger lightly along the edge. Biting her lip, she wondered if it would leave a deep cut.

"The water is getting higher!" Rachel was sounding more panicked by the minute. She'd picked a poor place to rest. The waves were breaking over the rock she was on.

Alex held her breath and slashed at the fishing line. With no handle, the metal of the blade dug into the flesh of Alex's hand.

"Help me!"

"Hold on, I'll be right there!" Alex worked as fast as she could, trying to ignore the pain shooting through her. Her hands shook, but she kept going, working the blade as best she could at the section of line that was still wrapped around Daredevil's flipper. If she could at least free that, he could swim and dive. He might stand a chance. Waves were brushing against her thighs now.

I can save them both. I can save them both. She kept repeating it in her head, hoping that would make it true. Daredevil twitched. Had she hurt him?

"It's okay, Daredevil. Shh," she murmured. Just a bit more and he might be able to get free.

"ALEX! The waves are pushing me!"

The crests of the waves were now lapping at Rachel's legs and she was weaving, trying to keep her balance. How long had Alex been working on Daredevil? She couldn't wait any longer.

Time was up.

Tears burned Alex's eyes. She'd done all she could.

Dropping the blade, she leaned forward, running her hands softly over Daredevil's head—the way she had the first time she'd seen him. "I'm sorry," she sobbed. "I tried, I really did. But I couldn't get it all off." She felt Daredevil stir beneath her hands.

The incoming tide was now high enough to float Daredevil and finally loosen him from his land prison. He bobbed gently in the current for a moment. Alex gasped as he tipped to one side. But then he righted himself, or the current pushed him back up. He began to drift away from her, out towards the open sea and his mom. Rooftop was still out by the rocks close to the mouth of the cove. It must have been too shallow for her to come closer.

"Bye, Daredevil," she whispered.

"ALEX!"

Rachel's scream spurred Alex to action. Ignoring her aching limbs, she fought the swirling current, forcing her exhausted body forward into deeper water to Rachel. Her pack floated beside her, its strap still across her shoulder.

She stumbled in the choppy waves, tripping over slippery rocks. Frigid ocean water sprayed up her nose and into her mouth. She squeezed her stinging eyes shut and coughed as the salty water burned its way down her throat.

Higher waves had splashed up, soaking Rachel's shorts. She was staggering against the onslaught of the tide to keep her balance, still clinging to her perch.

"I'll piggyback you," Alex gasped, finally reaching Rachel's side. Standing on the ocean floor, the water was now at her waist.

Rachel didn't say a word, but lunged at her with wild eyes.

Alex almost gagged as she was grabbed in a stranglehold. "Not so tight," she rasped, pulling Rachel's arms lower, away from her throat. "And let me turn around. Get on my back."

Rachel whimpered and Alex could feel her pressing her face into Alex's back.

Alex waded through the seaweed-clogged water. Her leg muscles were on fire. Her arms felt like they were being stabbed with a thousand needles. The salt water burned her cut hands like acid. She fixed her eyes on the rocky cliff.

The barking of the seals seemed to be encouragement to keep going. Or maybe they were laughing at her lame attempt to escape the relentless tide.

You can do it, sis. Just one more step. Adam's voice whispered inside her head.

Alex's foot slipped.

Suddenly, they were submerged in the icy water. Alex tried to push her head above the waves, but was pulled back down by two arms twisting like struggling snakes around her neck. Rachel was pulling her under.

Alex tugged frantically at Rachel's hands, but couldn't loosen her grip. Her lungs were going to explode! Again, she tried to push herself up out of the water. She needed air.

And again, Rachel dragged her down.

Desperate, Alex jabbed her elbow as hard as she could backward. Immediately, Rachel went limp. Alex surged upward, her head bursting through the waves. She sucked in a huge lungful of air.

"It's okay, Rachel," Alex panted. There was no answer. Alex couldn't feel Rachel behind her. She turned around.

Rachel wasn't there.

Alex held her breath and ducked below the surface. It was hard to see in the murky, swirling water. Large pieces of kelp drifted in front of her eyes. She swept them away. Rachel was there, floating just out of reach.

Alex lurched forward and grabbed Rachel's pink shirt, pulling her back. She hefted Rachel's head above the water and shook her.

"Rachel!" She shook her harder. "Rachel!"

Rachel coughed and opened her eyes, spitting out a mouthful of water. "I'm okay," she wheezed.

Alex tugged her along as she struggled the last few feet to the edge of the cliff. She grabbed onto a protruding ledge. Sagging with relief, she hugged tightly against the cliff as she tried to catch her breath. The waves were a constant beat against her back. Thankfully, the ground had sloped up a bit closer to shore, or they'd be under water by now.

Rachel was also clinging to the rocks—her head bowed and shoulders heaving as she sucked in large gulps of air.

Alex glanced upward. The seaweed wallpapered the rocks for at least fifteen feet above them. The tide wasn't even close to being done. They weren't safe here. "We've got to climb," Alex said.

"Please, Alex, can we wait? I don't think I can move."

"I know. I'm hurting too. But you see up there?" Alex pointed upward.

Rachel followed Alex's finger with her eyes. "Yeah."

"That's how high the water is going to be. If we don't climb right now, we'll die."

CHAPTER THIRTY-ONE

ALEX SCRAMBLED UP THE CLIFF as if Spike the German shepherd was nipping at her heels. Rachel somehow managed to keep pace behind her.

It felt as if they were climbing Mount Everest. Each new foothold was harder to grip, more slippery than the last one. Then something changed. It wasn't slippery anymore.

"Rachel," Alex said. "The seaweed's gone!"

"We're past where the tide comes up?"

"Yeah."

Rachel started to sob. "So, we're not going to die?"

"No, we're not going to die. C'mon, just a bit farther." Alex strained to pull herself up the last few feet. She reached down and grasped Rachel's hand.

They lay against the rocks. The only sounds were the ocean waves, their ragged breathing, and the barking seals out at sea. Alex scanned the ocean surface. The wall of fog was farther out now, past the entrance to the cove. She could see no trace of Rooftop and Daredevil. Where had they gone?

"I didn't think we'd make it," Rachel finally said.

"Really?"

"I don't know," Rachel murmured, staring off into the distance. "I was so scared. I mean, I can swim. But I couldn't do anything. What happened to me?"

"Fear does weird things to you," Alex said.

"I was thinking about my dad, you know? And that I wouldn't see him again. All I could think about was the last thing I did—yell at him that I didn't want a sister."

"You did?"

"Yeah. But…I guess a baby sister might be okay."

Alex leaned her head back against a grassy patch and closed her eyes. "Yeah, it might."

"I wish I was brave like you."

"Brave? Me?" Alex hadn't thought of it like that. She'd just done what she had to do. She wasn't brave, not by a long shot.

"You saved me. Sorry I tried to drown you," Rachel said in a small voice. "I was so scared. It didn't even seem like me, you know? Like I was watching everything from outside myself."

"I was scared too."

"You didn't show it."

"Sorry I jabbed you in the ribs." Alex played their escape back in her mind. It didn't seem like her, either. She'd done things she never imagined she could do. She certainly hadn't acted like the whimpering sap Adam used to drag around the woods.

"It hurts," Rachel said, rubbing her stomach. "But I'll take sore ribs over being dead any day."

Alex rolled over and stared at the ocean below. The

waves crashed against the cliff. There was still more tide to come in. There was still no sign of Daredevil or Rooftop, either.

She thought about how she'd yelled at Daredevil, saying he should have stayed with his mom. And how much like Adam he was. They didn't listen. What had made Daredevil leave the safety of his mother's side? For some reason, he had decided to do it, just like Adam had decided not to wear his helmet.

Adam knew he was supposed to wear his helmet. *I told him to wait, but he wouldn't,* she thought. *He decided not to wait. Just like Daredevil decided to leave his mother.* The realization washed over Alex like the rising tide had done. Everything came into perfect focus.

"It wasn't my fault."

"What?" Rachel's voice seemed far away.

"It wasn't my fault!"

"What wasn't?"

"My brother's accident!"

"Well, duh, of course not. I heard he skateboarded without his helmet. How could that be your fault?"

It was hard to explain it. The sadness she'd felt, the shame that she couldn't even get on the skateboard in front of his friends, the jealousy that he was so fearless…and all the other emotions had piled on top of her mountain of guilt—the guilt over having taken his helmet.

She'd been so mad, too. She remembered that. But he'd been lying in that bed, silent and still. How could she get mad at him? She'd felt guilty about that, too, and then angry at herself instead. She'd been smothered in a mammoth-sized boulder of guilt, so heavy it was a crushing weight on her all the time. And now it floated off her shoulders like a feather on the wind, disappearing as quickly as the fog they'd been wrapped in.

As they hobbled slowly back along the hiking trail to the lighthouse, it seemed to Alex like weeks rather than hours since she'd been on the rocks, building her inukshuk, then tearing it down. That anger seemed far away now too.

"I can't believe it's still the same day," Rachel mused, echoing Alex's thoughts.

"I know."

"I really have to pee!"

Alex shook her head. She was in the midst of a life-changing revelation and that's what Rachel came up with. "You're unbelievable."

"Well, I do!"

The path became more worn the closer they got to the lighthouse. Heat from the sunlight warmed their wet, shivering bodies.

"I'm really sorry about Daredevil, Alex."

"Me too." Alex automatically turned to survey the ocean again. Did he make it? Was Daredevil out there somewhere, swimming with his mom? She thought of the fishing line still wrapped around him. Was it possible he could escape it after the amount she'd cut free? He'd seemed so weak. "Maybe he'll be okay," she added hopefully.

"You never know," Rachel said. "I mean, it's always best to be positive, right?"

"Sure."

"I wonder if anybody missed us," Rachel said as they cut across the grass to Aunt Sophie's front door.

The house looked just the same. Bright blue curtains billowed out the open window. There was no car in the yard. Figures, Alex thought. They were probably off arguing somewhere and didn't even know she'd been gone. Aunt Sophie's car was gone, too—strange, since she almost never drove anywhere.

Rachel ran straight to the bathroom, leaving Alex in the messy kitchen. Coffee cups and plates were still scattered across the table. Marty was happily lapping from the cream jug. Where was everyone?

"Oh wow, are those Eva's cinnamon rolls?" Rachel said on her return. She didn't wait for an answer, pulling back the wrap and grabbing a fat bun from the pile. She stuffed a huge bite into her mouth and sat down with a groan. "Mmm."

Alex grabbed two pops from the fridge, passed one to Rachel, then pulled the tab off her own and tilted her head back. The cold liquid soothed her parched throat and she glugged it down all at once—just like they did on TV commercials.

Rachel did the same. "Ahh," she said, smacking her lips together. Then she let out a burp that would have made an ogre proud. "Oops!"

There was a crunch of tires on gravel and then car

doors slammed. Raised voices echoed from beside the house. The back door banged open. "I don't know what to do," Alex's mother wept. "Where else do we look? The man at the ferry was sure they wouldn't have gotten on without him noticing…"

"It's all right, Colleen, we'll find them," Alex's dad said.

They stood in the hallway. Her dad had his arms around her mom and she had her head on his shoulder.

"We can't lose her, Douglas," her mom said, her voice muffled by her dad's shirt. "Not her too!"

"She's okay," her dad said reassuringly.

Alex felt like she'd been transported to some kind of alternate universe. These were her parents, but not really her parents. She should have said something. But she was frozen in shock.

"Are you looking for us?" Rachel piped up.

Her mother spun around. "Alex!" she cried, running towards her. Then she stopped, gasping. "What happened to you?"

"What do you mean?"

Her mother reached out and lightly touched her face. "You look like someone beat you up." She turned to Rachel. "So do you. Were you two fighting?" she frowned.

"No, but—"

"And you're soaking wet!"

"It's a long story. We were—"

Her mom wrapped her arms around her and squeezed her tightly. "I thought something had happened to you!"

"We almost died," Rachel said, "seriously."

"I'm okay, Mom," Alex said. She hugged her back. "I'm okay, now."

"We'll work things out. We will…"

Her dad came over and put his arms around them both. "Alex, you're the most important thing in the world to us," he muttered gruffly.

Standing there, soaking wet, in the embrace of her parents, another one of those pieces of her that had felt disconnected quietly slipped back into place.

They stood like that for a moment, and then her mom gently pulled back. "What does she mean, you almost died?"

Alex and Rachel exchanged glances. Rachel shrugged and took another bite of Eva's cinnamon bun. Alex was on her own.

"Uh," Alex began. How was she going to explain this one? Then she realized it didn't matter. She felt a peacefulness inside her, free from guilt. For the first time in a very long time, Alex had an overwhelming feeling that things were going to be okay.

EPILOGUE

"MOM, YOUR SUIT LOOKS GREAT," Alex said. "Just like the last two you tried on. Come on, we're going to be late."

"I'm almost ready," her mom said, pulling the top off that she was wearing and grabbing another one off the hanger.

Alex sighed. You'd think her mom was the one getting married.

"What are you doing up there? Having surgery? Let's go!" Aunt Sophie's impatient cry echoed up from the bottom floor.

Alex bounded down the stairs, her gift tucked safely in her bag. "She's coming," she said to Aunt Sophie.

"She does know this is a country wedding?" Aunt Sophie rolled her eyes. "Not some royal event in the big city?"

"You can tell her," Alex smirked. "Is it really on Gus's boat?"

"That's what he said."

Alex took the fresh eggs Aunt Sophie had just collected and began placing them in the egg tray in the door of the fridge. "I thought Eva got seasick."

"Yes, it should be interesting."

Aunt Sophie slipped her feet into flat sandals. She was wearing a short-sleeved flowery top and white walking shorts.

Alex smoothed the front of her purple skort. Even though there were shorts underneath, it felt too much like a skirt for her liking.

"Don't fidget, it looks nice," her mom said from the stairs.

There was a bounce in her mom's step and she was smiling. Her hair was cut short in a new style with highlights. "You look like a model, Mom."

Her mom blushed and giggled like a kid. "Oh, stop."

"She's right," Aunt Sophie said. "The pink in that outfit is a great colour on you."

"What a cheering section you two are!" Her mom grabbed her purse. "Do you think we'll need jackets?"

"The middle of August is pretty warm here," Aunt Sophie said. "But it gets cool on the water. I'd take one, just in case."

Her mom was humming under her breath as she swept out the door ahead of them.

"She's acting like she's going on a date," Aunt Sophie whispered to Alex as they followed her mom out the door.

"Dad's going to be there," Alex whispered back.

"Yeah, I know."

"She's been on the phone with him almost every night this week from Nan's house." It was like her parents were dating—a bit weird, but nice-weird.

Her mom had whisked her away to Nan's in Bridgewater after her almost-drowning day six weeks ago, vowing to watch her every second, keep her totally safe, blah, blah. At first, when her dad came to see her, he'd pick her up and they'd go out. Then, a few times, he'd stay and have dinner with all of them. Lately, she'd heard Mom talking to him on the phone and she'd invited him to come to the wedding. And there had been no fighting. Now here it was the end of August, and they were back on the island.

They strolled down through the village to the dock. The *Evania Rose* was already packed with guests. Her dad smiled and waved from a far corner, pinned in by an older couple.

Rachel came bursting out of the cabin. "Finally!" she said. "I've been waiting for you forever." She hopped over the steps and looped her arm through Alex's. "And you wore purple."

"Well, you emailed me to say I had to," Alex said. "But no one else is. I thought it was a theme or something."

"Kind of," Rachel said. She leaned closer. "It's a surprise."

"For who?"

"You'll see." Rachel tugged her on board. "Come check out the cake—it's awesome!"

Inside the glassed-in cabin area, purple and yellow streamers were draped around the windows. Balloons with hearts on them were tied to chairs and swayed gently back and forth. The research books had been removed and the table was covered in a white cloth. Sandwiches of all different kinds were arranged on lettuce-lined trays, garnished with tiny tomatoes and little cubes of cheese. Alex spied a plate of ham and cheese rolls.

"Isn't it beautiful?" Rachel pointed to the centrepiece—

a two-tiered cake covered in purple and yellow roses. "I helped Eva decorate it."

Alex grinned. It was pretty obvious to her which flowers Eva had made and which were Rachel's creations. "Wow! Great job."

"Thanks," Rachel beamed. "I helped make the punch, too. Try some."

"Hey, no snacking," a gruff voice teased.

"You shaved off your beard!" Rachel squealed. "You look very handsome, Uncle Gus."

Gus was standing in the doorway to the wheelhouse, dressed in a white shirt and black pants. It looked like he had attempted to tame his wild mane of hair, but hadn't been very successful. He was definitely still very lion-like.

"Thanks, squirt." Gus reached out as if to ruffle her hair.

"Hey, watch it. Mom took me to the hairdresser."

"Pardon me," Gus laughed. "Nice to see you, Alex. My two spotters, together again."

Spotters—Alex felt a sinking in her stomach as she thought about Daredevil. "Have you been out on tours?" she asked, hoping for news.

"No." He shook his head. "Eva's had me all over the place, introducin' me to relatives and such. I've cut back this month quite a bit and my brother's boy has been running all the tours for me."

"Oh. I kept checking your blog from my Nan's, but there weren't any updates." There hadn't been any mention of either Rooftop or her calf in any of the other whale-watch blogs, either.

Gus patted her shoulder. "Wonderin' about your little friend, I s'pose," he said kindly. "I know how you felt about him. We did search for him, but there was no sign. Given the state you told me he was in, still tangled in fishing line, and how long he'd been beached…"

"I know," Alex said. "It's just, well, I was still hoping—"

"Nothin' wrong with a little hope," Gus agreed.

"No gloomies today, Alex," Rachel said. "Eva, let's open the gifts first."

Eva beamed at them from the doorway. "Why not? We can do whatever we want. May as well have a spot of lunch while we're at it."

"Great idea," Alex said. She'd had enough gloom and doom. Besides, she was excited for them to open their presents too.

Looking a bit confused that the gift opening and lunch were coming before the ceremony, guests were nevertheless quick to adjust and hit the food table in the cabin. Laden down with sandwiches and punch, everyone found seats while Gus and Eva opened their gifts. Alex had made sure hers was on top.

"Bogs, that's beautiful!" Gus said in his booming voice. "That Alex has some talent, doesn't she, Eva?"

"Must run in the family," Eva said. "Sophie's got such a fine hand herself."

"Show us," Rachel said.

Eva turned the frame around to everyone. The coloured pencil sketch of Eva's exotic flower garden was a wild splash of colours.

"Wow," Rachel cooed, "you *are* good! Can you do one of me?"

Alex blushed. "I'm not so good at doing people yet."

"That's okay. I'll be your practice person."

Alex glanced out one of the large windows. The ocean was as calm as glass. A flock of orange-beaked puffins floated quietly nearby. At one point Alex saw her dad reach over and take her mom's hand. And her mom didn't pull away this time. That was a good sign.

After lunch, the small crowd of twenty remained in the cabin, chatting with Eva and Gus. It was almost time for the ceremony, which was to take place on the open deck. As Gus relayed one of his stories to the minister and guests, Alex drifted outside to the back of the boat. Alone, she kneeled on the cushioned bench. She leaned over the side, holding her arms close to the water as she'd done that first day she'd met Daredevil.

"Are you out there?" she whispered, knowing in her heart that he wouldn't come. Not a ripple broke the shimmering smoothness. She stared into the deep blue depths, imagining she could see both of them together— Adam, her daredevil brother, whooping in glee as he flew along on his skateboard, and Daredevil, the baby whale, zooming in circles around him. Alex reached down to dip her hand in the water, watching the ripples fan outward.

She was glad she'd gone to the lighthouse when they arrived that morning. It was something she'd thought about often since leaving the island. It had felt good rebuilding the inukshuk—the symbol of her family. She'd even included a stone for Daredevil this time. He and Adam were the two foundation stones—her two daredevils.

"Are you ready, Alex?"

Alex turned to look at Eva. "You look beautiful, Eva." She wore a lilac pantsuit with shiny silver sandals. "But I thought you got seasick. You don't look sick at all."

"Seasick patch," Eva said, tapping behind her ear. "Figured my namesake was the perfect place for the wedding."

Alex nodded. It did seem like the perfect place. Rachel smiled at her as she approached from the cabin.

"Now, are you ready to be a flower girl?" Eva asked.

"Flower girl?"

"Didn't Rachel tell you?" Eva raised an eyebrow. "Flower girl...Hmm, I guess you're too old for that, aren't you? How about bridesmaid, then?"

Alex didn't know what to say.

"Don't worry," Rachel said. "I took care of everything." Rachel dragged Eva and Alex back into the cabin.

"Took care of what?" Alex asked, confused.

"The flowers weren't murdered." Rachel lifted the edge of the tablecloth and pulled out potted Gerbera daisies from underneath. "See? They're alive!" She thrust one of the satin-wrapped pots at Alex.

"I was told you had a problem with cut flowers," Eva murmured, her eyes twinkling.

Alex laughed so hard she thought she'd burst. She was still laughing when they marched out of the cabin holding their flowerpots filled with daisies and dirt and stepped into the sunlight.

ACKNOWLEDGEMENTS

To James—our wonderful trips to Brier Island were the inspiration for the setting of this story.

Thanks to my writing group members past and present, The Scribblers—Daphne Greer, Lisa Harrington, Graham Bullock, Jennifer Thorne, Joanna Butler, and Cynthia d'Entremont. Hanging tight through thick and thin, we are in this together.

To my amazing friends and family, who have taken on the jobs of test readers, marketers, or both, thanks for everything. You are the best cheering section anyone could wish for, especially Lisa Smith, Sandy Denny, Rhonda Basden, Margaret Laidlaw (Aunt Peg), Susan Jain, Anne Marie Long, Mom, Dad, David, Shari, Paulette, and Will.

And to Diane, Terrilee, and Penelope—you are a great team.